Benjamin Leopold Farjeon

Miser Farebrother

A Novel: Vol. I.

Benjamin Leopold Farjeon

Miser Farebrother
A Novel: Vol. I.

ISBN/EAN: 9783337066482

Printed in Europe, USA, Canada, Australia, Japan

Cover: Foto ©Andreas Hilbeck / pixelio.de

More available books at **www.hansebooks.com**

MISER FAREBROTHER.

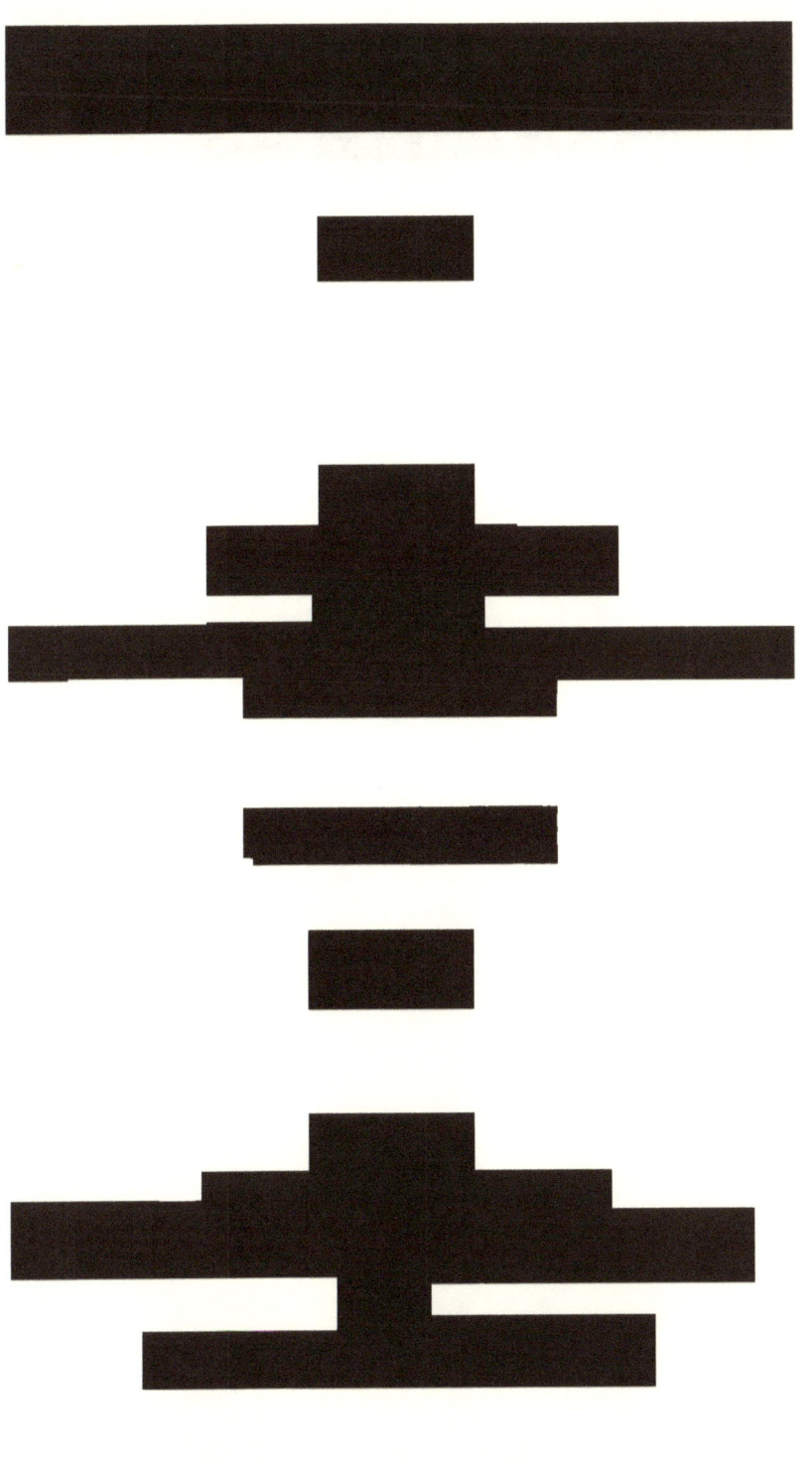

CONTENTS.

MISER FAREBROTHER.

-——:o:——

CHAPTER I.

THE LAST OF THE CARE-TAKERS.

IN Dropmore Beeches, near Beddington, county of Surrey, stands a red brick mansion, in the Gothic style, known as Parksides. It is situated on the outskirts of an estate of forty acres, comprised of a few acres of cover, and, for the rest, of shrubberies, meadow-land, and a wilderness wood, upon the arrangement of which great care had been bestowed and a vast amount of money expended. This was in the old days, when the house had been occupied by a family of good standing, the heirs of which had resided in it for many generations. Pride was taken in it then, and it was deservedly renowned for its beauty. The country people round about quoted Parksides as a possession which reflected honour upon themselves, and the vicarious distinction was accounted of high value. They had good reasons for being proud of it, and of its masters and mistresses, who were to the fore not only in the county but in the metropolis. The gentlemen fought for King and country, and administered the laws; the ladies dispensed charities and set the fashions; they attended Court, hunted, travelled, and held their heads high, as was their due. But other times, other men. The family that had owned Parksides for centuries slipped out of the ranks—for which they had none but themselves to blame. A strain of foreign blood was introduced by marriage, and the heir born of that union inherited the vices of his mother's family. He ran his course merrily; and after him a spendthrift heir, and after him another, reaped what had been bred and zealously cultivated in the bone. They played the part of absentees, and plunged into the fashionable dissipations of the city—raked, and made matches on the race-courses, rattled the dice-box from night till morning, were always ready for any mad prank, drank deeply, and borrowed at exorbitant inte-

rest—until they had thoroughly succeeded in squandering
their fortune. It was too late, then, for repentance : Parksides was lost to them and theirs for ever. There had been
long and complicated law proceedings in connection with
the estate, and at the period of the opening of this story it
was supposed to be in Chancery—which troubled itself not
at all in the matter—and to have no rightful or legal
owner. Nevertheless, it was occupied by a man who had
earned the name of Miser Farebrother, who paid rent to
no one, and was not called upon to do so. It was really
doubtful whether any person had authority to demand it ;
and if a claimant had come forward, his right would have
been stubbornly contested by Miser Farebrother, who had
papers in his fire proof safe proving, in some entangled way,
that he had advanced money upon the estate which entitled
him to possession. The lawyers, for a great number of
years, had gathered rich harvests out of Parksides, and,
after picking its bones clean and involving it in legal com-
plications which the entire learned profession could not
have unravelled, had turned their backs upon it and flown
to more profitable game. Its fate, long before it fell into

the hands of Miser Farebrother, may be described in one word—decay. The wilderness wood, the wild charms of which had been preserved with much care and skill, was so encumbered with stunted wood growth and overrun with giant weeds that it resembled a miniature Forest of Despair; the shrubberies were wrecks; the meadow-land was thick with tufts of rank grass; and the only part of the estate which had thriven was the cover, in which the rabbits literally swarmed, spreading destruction all around. Not a shilling did Miser Farebrother expend upon the grounds— a proof that he did not regard his rights as absolutely in-contestable. He had a keen eye for the main chance, and money could have been laid out on the land with profit, both in the present and the future; but he was not the man to waste the smallest coin upon a doubtful venture. "Safe and sure" had been his motto all through his life, and from a worldly point of view he had made it pay.

He took possession of Parksides in the dead of night. For at least a dozen years it had been without a tenant, and for many years before that time its only inmates had been the care-takers appointed by the Courts and the lawyers.

The last of these care-takers were a very old man and a very old woman of the name of Barley, who were supposed to have died of starvation in the house. It was said that there were long arrears of wages due to them, which were never paid, because the last shilling of the available funds had been swept away by wig and gown. No one cared to assume responsibility in the matter, and so this old couple were left in possession to do as they pleased. They had come from a distance to enter upon their duties, and nobody in the neighbourhood knew anything about them or their antecedents; nor was it known how they came to be appointed. That they were the poorest of the poor was clear —all that they brought with them to Parksides were a stick and a bundle. The old man carried the stick, and the old woman the bundle.

How they subsisted was a mystery. In the autumn they were in the habit of picking up bits of broken branches and carrying them into the house, presumably to serve in lieu of coals when winter came on. Both of them were bent nearly double with old age and rheumatism. Occasionally they would be seen sitting on a log, very close to each other, with a little pile of stones before them, which they shied with weak and trembling hands at a rabbit or a bird, or at shadows which they mistook for living creatures. They never by any chance hit anything they aimed at, and they did not even succeed in frightening the birds or the rabbits, which darted hither and thither and hopped about quite near to them in the most unconcerned fashion. During the latter years of their tenancy one or other of the old people would sometimes be seen, when the weather was fine, creeping out of Parksides and out of Beddington, starting early in the morning and returning late at night. On these occasions it was observed that they carried a parcel, which without further evidence it was decided was something abstracted from the mansion, which they were travelling to a distance to sell, in order to obtain food; and it was also decided that they did not dispose of these articles in the immediate neighbourhood of Beddington, lest they should be accused of theft. If this were really the case, the old couple might have dismissed their fears; the difficulty of finding a prosecutor would have been insurmountable; and as to portable property of a sufficiently small size to be tied up in a pocket handkerchief, there was little enough of that in the mansion. All that was valuable and of easy carriage had long since been seized and sold, lawfully or unlawfully. The ruin of Parksides was not a grand crash, in the thunder of which lightning-flashes of old glories made themselves visible; it was a long and mean decline, made up of piecemeal borrowings and bit-by-bit sales; of filchings and small robberies, a few feathers by this sharp rogue, a few feathers by that, from the plumage of the birds that were once the pride of the country. There was certainly plenty of old furniture in the house, which had been allowed to remain, probably because it was heavy and cumbersome and falling to pieces —bedsteads, tables, chairs, benches and sideboards, quaintly and curiously carved; rich tapestries too, mostly worn to shreds, and rotted by age and neglect, in which old stories had been woven by fair hands. They and the gallant deeds they recorded were now on an equality; the reflected radiance of stately seasons of honourable life and dignified labour was utterly and for ever dead, leaving no soul behind; the story was told, and flesh and silk were little better than dust. There were not any pictures in frames in the rooms;

but there were paintings on the wall panels, so faded now and colourless that the learning of an antiquary were needed to describe them.

Amidst these ancient surroundings the last of the care-takers, old Mr. and Mrs. Barley, moved and starved. One can imagine them creeping up the wide staircases, and tottering about the rooms, living ghosts, clinging to each other for support (they were both past seventy, and chronically weak from want of proper nourishment), wondering whether they had not reached the dead world upon the brink of which they stood. There came a hard winter, and a fall of snow which lasted intermittently, but pretty steadily, nevertheless, for a full fortnight. It was during this winter that an incident occurred in the career of the last of the care-takers.

Said a gossip to a kindred heart, trudging through the snow at least a hundred yards for the purpose, "My man, coming home from work last night, passed the gates of Parksides."

"He does always, doesn't he?" was the response, evincing in the querist an ungracious spirit, for Gossip Number Two was aware that her neighbour had not walked ankle-deep in the coldest of carpets to impart this information.

"Yes, he does always, when he doesn't go another way."

"What other way?"

"The way of the Hog in the Pound." (For comprehension to uninformed minds, a public-house.)

"That's the way he likes best," observed Gossip Number Two, still with the ungracious spirit upon her.

"*You* needn't boast," said Gossip Number One; "your man leaves half his wages there."

"Yes; worse luck! But what about Parksides?"

"He saw a woman going in."

"Old Mrs. Barley?"

"No; a youngish woman, looking like a beggar, with a boy holding on to her."

"A tramp! The Barleys can't help her—can't help themselves."

"She asked my man whether that was Parksides, and whether a married couple of the name of Barley lived there. 'Lives there!' says my man to her. 'Starves there, would be nearer the truth.' The woman gave a sigh, and passed into the grounds."

"Is that all?" asked Gossip Number Two, disappointed in a story so bare of incident.

"That's all," replied Gossip Number One. "Leastways it's all my man told me."

"It ain't much."

"No, it ain't. But," added Gossip Number One, cheerfully illogical, her temperament being livelier than that of her neighbour, "what can we expect in such weather? Just look how the snow's coming down again!"

This shifting of responsibility from a colourless story to a remarkable storm—which, despite its inconveniences, was interesting because it afforded a sound theme for conversation—somewhat mollified Gossip Number Two, who, accompanied by her visitor, stepped to the window to gaze upon the whirling flakes. They were thick and heavy, and a strong, uncertain wind was lashing them furiously about, this way and that, with a bewildering lack of method which furnished an exception to the indisputable truth that order is nature's first law. The window through which the gossips were looking was in the front room of the cottage, and faced the narrow lane which led to the main road. Along this lane a woman was walking, with a little boy scarcely three years of age tugging at her gown. Presently they reached the cottage, where the woman paused to wipe the snow from her face and eyes. She was very poorly dressed, and belonged evidently to the lower orders.

"Is that her?" asked Gossip Number Two.

"It might be. She's got a little boy with her, and she looks like a beggar. Let's have her in."

Candour compels the admission that it was not an instinct of hospitality or humanity that prompted the suggestion. It was simply curiosity to discover what connection existed between the poor woman and her child and old Mr. and Mrs. Barley.

There was not much to learn. The last of the care-takers were her parents. Having lost her husband, and being at her wits' end how to live, she had tramped a matter of sixty miles to Parksides in the hope that her parents might be able to assist her. Her hope was shattered the moment she saw them. So desperate were their circumstances that she would stop with them only one night, and she was now on her way back to her native town, in which, at all events, she had a claim upon the poor-house. She did not complain. She had been so used to poverty and hardships that she harboured them without a murmur, but she said it was bitter weather, and she did not know how ever she would get home again. While she was telling her tale, sitting by the fireside—for the warmth of which she expressed herself humbly thankful—the little fellow in her lap fell asleep.

" What is his name ? "

" Tom—after his poor father," said the woman.

Gossip Number One looked at Gossip Number Two, who nodded, and going to the cupboard took therefrom a teapot, a tea-caddy, and a loaf of bread. A full kettle was steaming on the hob. As the woman raised her head, her hostess saw tears glistening in her eyes.

" There, there, my dear," she said, " we none of us know what we may come to. A cup of tea 'll warm your inside. And, I declare ! it's left off snowing again ! "

Half an hour afterward the woman, having thanked her entertainers, resumed her journey, and the gossips stood on the doorstep and gazed at her vanishing form until a turn in the narrow lane hid her from their sight. Comforting food and human sympathy had strengthened her, and she was carrying her child, who, as his mother declared, was almost "dead with sleep." Strange and sub.le are the invisible links which connect life with life and already one was spiritually forged between the slumbering lad and men and women who will play their parts in this story of human love and passion and suffering and desire.

In the ancient decayed house yonder old Mr. and Mrs. Barley were talking in quavering tones of their Jane, who had paid them her last earthly visit.

"She'll marry agin, mother, will our Jane," piped the old man ; "she was always a taking lass. It's only yesterday she was in pinafores."

For three years longer the Barleys remained tenants of Parksides, and then departed for another bourne. It was bruited about the neighbourhood that they had been found dead in the kitchen, clasped in each other's arms. So little had been seen of them during the last years of their tenancy that but small interest had been taken in them. They troubled nobody, and nobody troubled them. But being dead, the case was different ; popular fancy placed them on a pinnacle, and they became distinguished.

"So the Barleys have gone," was said. "Who'll be the next ?"

No records are to hand throwing light upon what was done with their bodies ; among the uninformed the general belief was that they were not buried, but that they "dis-appeared." Of course their spirits remained, to the comfort of superstitious souls still in the flesh. There was a talk of "ghosts," and the ball, being set rolling, grew apace. The natural consequence was that Parksides acquired the reputa-tion of being a haunted house. The ghosts of the old people were seen by many persons of all ages—who were ready to testify to the same in the witness box—standing at the windows, or moving familiarly about the grounds, or seated on the roof top ; always very lovingly arm in arm. Not in the memory of the oldest inhabitant had such an enjoyable excitement been furnished, and the superstition caused Parksides to be avoided at night-time. Those who

were fearsomely courageous enough to make a special excur-
sion to "see the ghosts" always went in company, and
always came back with white faces and trembling limbs.
Children would huddle together in a shrinking heap, standing so for a few minutes, and then, startled into active
movement by a sudden cry from one among them, would
scream : "There they are ! Oh ! oh ! They're coming
after us ! " and would scamper off as fast as their legs would
carry them ; until, at a safe distance, they would pause,
breathless, to compare notes.

Here was a chance for the imagination, and it ran riot.
No speculation was too extravagant.

"Did *you* see them ? *I* did ! What did they look like ?
Like what they are, you dunce—ghosts ! Old Barley had a
nightcap on. So had she. They were all in white. He was
smoking a pipe. Did you see the fire coming out of his
mouth ? He blew it at us. Yes, and when they saw we
didn't go away they got up, and grew and grew till they
were higher than the trees ! Johnny, come home with me
to mother, She wouldn't believe *me* when I told her. Oh,
didn't they look awful ! "

Uninteresting as old Mr. and Mrs. Barley had been during their lifetime, it cannot be denied that their ghosts supplied an entertainment better than any theatre.

CHAPTER II.

THIS condition of affairs favoured Miser Farebrother, when,
in pursuance of a cunningly-formed plan, he took possession of the estate. Already he claimed to have a hold
upon it, and who had a better right than he to live there
rent free? There was a fascination in the prospect. To
live rent free! To have a house and land all one's own!
There would be a claim for Queen's taxes, perhaps, and
rates. Well he would pay a little—as little as possible.
The government receipts would go a long way to strengthen
his hold upon the property. The rent of his house in
London was ruinous. In so many years he would be so
much money in pocket—a fortune. Then, he had heard
and read that if a man lived in a house for a certain time
without paying rent, it became legally and lawfully his own,

to sell or do what he liked with. It was a bold step, but the prize was so valuable that he would risk it.

He made two preliminary investigations of the property, and as everything depended upon secrecy, these visits were paid in the night when nobody was about. He knew nothing of the popular belief that the place was haunted.

On the first of these visits he was undisturbed. He crept into the grounds within a few minutes of midnight, and made his way to a back door. It yielded to his touch. He lit a candle which he had brought with him, and entered. All was still and lonely; not a sound reached his ears; there was not a crumb in the mansion upon which even a rat or a mouse could live. Stealthily and warily he made a tour of the rooms, shading the light with his hand when he was near a window. There was small need for such a precaution, but he took it, nevertheless.

"Safe and sure!" he muttered—"safe and sure!"

He was gratified and amazed to discover so many pieces of old furniture in the house; and he made out a list upon paper of what it would be necessary to bring with him when he actually took possession : his desk, containing his private papers and account-books, in which were entered his precious transactions ; a few pots and pans, and some sheets and blankets ; the personal clothing his wife would attend to. These things could be put into a cart, and a single horse would be sufficient to convey them from London. He had ascertained the distance—between fifteen and sixteen miles. He and his wife and child could ride in the cart. So much saved !

Determining to come again before the final step was taken, he left the house at two in the morning as secretly and quietly as he had entered it.

His second visit was paid in the course of the following week, at about the same hour of the night. He entered the house, again without being disturbed, and lighting his candle, made another tour of the rooms. He stood in one which had been a principal bedroom, and he resolved to turn it to the same use. On this occasion he made a more careful examination of the furniture, which, in consequence of the craze for the antique, he knew to be worth a great deal of money ; and he was rubbing his hands with glee, having placed the candle on a table, and was thinking, "All mine! all mine!" when a sound from the bedstead almost drove the blood from his heart. It was a sound of soft breathing.

He stood for a few moments transfixed; his tongue clave to the roof of his mouth; his feet seemed fastened to the floor. The sound of soft, regular breathing continued, and presently, as nothing more alarming occurred, he began to recover himself. His feet became loosened, his limbs regained their power of action. Noiselessly he took from his pockets two articles—one a revolver, which he always carried about him; the other a bottle of water. He moistened his throat, and returned the bottle to his pocket; and then, holding the pistol, without any distinct idea of the use he might put it to, he tremblingly approached the bed. There, fully dressed, lay a lad of some thirteen or fourteen years of age.

A common-looking lad, sleeping very peacefully and calmly.

Miser Farebrother, seeing before him an enemy whom he could easily overcome, shook the lad roughly, and cried, "Now, then, what are you doing here?"

The lad jumped up, and slid from the bed to the floor.

"Do you hear me?" cried Miser Farebrother. "What are you doing here, you vagabond?"

That the lad was terribly frightened was clear by his movements; he shrank back and cowered at the sight of the pistol, but he managed to blurt out:

"I ain't doing no harm, your honour! I'm only having a sleep."

"How dare you sleep here?" demanded Miser Farebrother, in a tone of authority. "You have come to commit a robbery—to rob *me*! I'll put you in jail for it."

"Don't your honour—don't!" pleaded the lad, still cowering and shrinking. "I ain't done a morsel of harm—upon my soul I ain't! I didn't come here to steal nothink—upon my soul I didn't!"

Miser Farebrother put the pistol into his pocket, and the lad began to whimper.

"Do you know I could take your life, could lawfully take it," said Miser Farebrother, "for breaking into *my* house as you have done, and sleeping upon *my* bed?"

"Yes, your honour; but please don't! I didn't brea'c into the house. The door was open."

"Stop that crying."

"Yes, your honour."

And the lad, in default of a handkerchief, dug his knuckles into his eyes. A lad of resource and some decision of character, he cried no more. This fact was not lost upon Miser Farebrother.

"You did not break into the house, you say?"

"No, your honour; upon my soul I didn't!"

"And you found the door open?"

"Yes, your honour."

"Which door?"

"The kitchen door, your honour."

"How long have you been here?"

"Three days, your honour."

This piece of information rather confounded Miser Farebrother, who, himself an interloper, was feeling his way; but he was politic enough not to betray himself.

"Three days, eh—and not yet caught?"

"Nobody wants to ketch me, your honour."

"Not your father and mother?"

"Ain't got none, your honour."

"Somebody else, then, in their place?"

"There ain't nobody in their place. There ain't a soul that's got a call to lay a hand upon me."

"Except me."

"Yes, your honour," said the lad, humbly: "but I didn't know."

His complete subservience and humbleness had an effect upon Miser Farebrother. He judged others by himself—a common enough standard among mortals—and he was not the man to trust to mere words; but there was a semblance of truth in the manner of the lad which staggered him. In all England it would have been difficult to find a man less given to sentiment, and less likely to be led by it, but the lad's conspicuous helplessness, and his ingenuous blue eyes —which, now that the pistol was put away, looked frankly at the miser—no less than his own scheme of taking possession of Parksides by stealth and in secrecy, were elements. in favour of this lad, so strangely found in so strange a situation. A claim upon Parksides Miser Farebrother un-

doubtedly possessed ; he held papers, in the shape of liens
u on complicated mortgages, which he had purchased for
a song ; but he had something more than a latent suspicion
that the law's final verdict was necessary to establish the
validity and exact value of his claim.   This he had not
sought to obtain, knowing that it would have led him into
ruinous expense and probable failure.   These circumstances
. were the breeders of an uneasy consciousness that he and
the lad, in their right to occupy Parksides, were somewhat
upon an equality.   Hence it was necessary to be cautious,
and to feel his way, as it were.

"Where are your people ? " he asked.

The lad stared at him.

"My people ! "

"Your people," repeated Miser Farebrother.   "Where
you live, you know."

"Ain't got no people," said the lad.   " Don't live nowhere."

" Listen to me, you young scoundrel," said Miser Farebrother, shaking a menacing forefinger at him ; " if you're
trying to impose upon me by a parcel of lies, you'll find

yourself in the wrong box. As sure as I'm the master of this house, I'll have you locked up and fed upon stones and water for the rest of your life."

" I ain't trying to impose upon you," persisted the lad, speaking very earnestly ; " I ain't telling you a parcel of lies. Look here, your honour, have you got a book ? "

" What book ? "

" I don't care what book—any book ! Give it me, and I'll kiss it, and swear on it that I've told you the truth, the whole truth, and nothing but the truth."

" You'll have to tell something more of yourself before I've done with you. Where did you live before you lived nowhere ? "

" Hailsham, your honour."

" Where's that ? "

" Don't know, your honour."

" How far from here ? "

" Six days, your honour."

" None of your nonsense. How far ? "

" Couldn't tell to a yard, if you was to skin me alive. It took me six days to git here."

" You walked ? "

" Yes, your honour ; every step of the way."

" Who did you live with at Hailsham ? "

" Mother."

" You said you had none."

" More I have.   She's dead."

" Father too ? "

" Yes ; ever so long ago."

" What brought you here ? "

" My legs."

Miser Farebrother restrained his anger—for which there was no sound reason, the lad's manner being perfectly respectful.

" What did you come here for ? "

" To see grandfather.   I heerd mother talk of him and grandmother ever so many times, and that they lived down here ; so when she was buried I thought I might do worse than come and see 'em."

" Have you seen them ? "

" No, your honour ; they're dead too."   The lad added, mournfully, " Everybody's dead, I think."

" They lived down here, you say ? "

" Yes; 'most all their lives; in this fine house. They was taking care of it for the master."

Some understanding of the situation dawned upon Miser Farebrother, and a dim idea that it might be turned to his use and profit.

" What was their name ? "

" Barley, your honour. That's my name, Tom Barley; and if you'd give me a job I'd be everlastingly thankful."

Miser Farebrother, with his eyes fixed upon the lad's face, into which, in the remote prospect of a job, a wistful expression had stolen, considered for a few moments. Here was a lad who knew nobody in the neighbourhood and whom nobody knew, and who recognized in him the master of Parksides. In a few days he intended to enter into occupation, and he had decided not to bring a servant with him. Tom Barley would be useful, and was, indeed, just the kind of person he would have chosen to serve him in a rough way—a stranger, whose only knowledge of him was that he was the owner of Parksides; and no fear of blabbing, having nothing to blab about. He made up his mind.

He took a little book from his pocket, the printed text of which was the calculation of interest upon ten pounds and upward for a day, for a week, for a month, for a year, at from five to fifty per cent. per annum.

"Take this book in your hand and swear upon it that you have told me the truth."

Tom Barley kissed the interest book solemnly, and duly registered the oath.

"If I take you into my service," said Miser Farebrother, "will you serve me faithfully?"

A sudden light of joy shone in Tom Barley's eyes. "Give me the book again, your honour, and I'll take my oath on it."

"No," said Miser Farebrother. As a matter of fact, he had been glad to get the book back in his possession, not knowing yet whether Tom Barley could read, and being fearful that he might open it and discover its nature; "I'll be satisfied with your promise. But you can't sleep in the house, you know."

"There's places outside, your honour; there's one where the horses was. That'll be good enough for me."

"Quite good enough. How much money have you got?"

"I had a penny when I reached here, your honour, but it's gone. I spent it in bread."

"Is that all you've had to eat?"

"No, your honour; I killed a rabbit."

"Very well. I take you into my service, Tom Barley. Twopence a week, and you sleep outside. When you're a man I'll make your fortune if you do as you're told. What's to-day?"

"Monday, your honour," said Tom Barley, now completely happy. "The church bells was ringing yesterday."

"On Thursday night," said Miser Farebrother, "at between twelve and one o'clock, I shall be here with a cart. There will be a lady in it besides me, and—and—a child. You understand?"

"Yes, your honour, I'm awake."

"Be awake then, wide awake, or you will get in trouble. I shall want you to help get some things out of the cart. There will be a moon, and you will be able to see me drive up. Look out for me. Here's a penny on account of your first week's wages. You can buy some more bread with it, and if you like you can kill another rabbit. Was it good?"

"Prime, your honour."

"It ought to be. It was *my* rabbit, you know, Tom Barley, and you'll kill no more than one between now and Thursday. The skins are worth money, and many a man's been hanged for stealing them. You will not forget?—Thursday night between twelve and one."

"No fear of my forgetting, your honour," said Tom Barley, ducking his head in obeisance; "I shall be here, wide-awake, waiting for you."

Miser Farebrother saw Tom Barley out of the house, and walked away through the shadows, rubbing his hands in satisfaction at having done a good night's work.

CHAPTER III.

AT the appointed hour a cart drew up at the gates of Park-sides, in which, in addition to the driver, were Miser Fare-brother and his wife and child. Tom Barley was waiting for them, and he darted forward to assist. Miser Fare-brother alighted first, and receiving the child from his wife, looked rather helplessly about him, Mrs. Farebrother not being strong enough to alight without help.

"Can you hold a child?" asked Miser Farebrother of Tom Barley.

"Yes, your honour," replied Tom, eagerly; and he took the child, a little girl scarcely two years old, and cuddled it close to him.

The mother looked anxiously at the lad, and the moment her feet touched the ground she relieved him of the charge

The moonlight shone upon the group, and Tom Barley gazed in wonder at the lady's beautiful face and the pretty babe. Desiring Tom to assist the driver in the removal of the necessary household articles he had brought with him in the cart, Miser Farebrother led the way into the house, which they entered through the door at the back. As he was lighting a candle, Mrs. Farebrother sighed and shivered.

"It is very lonely," she murmured.

"It is very comfortable," he retorted; "a palace compared to the place we have left. You will get well and strong here."

She shook her head, and said, in a tone so low that the words did not reach her husband's ears, "I shall never get well."

"What is that you say?" he cried, sharply. She did not reply. "Instead of grumbling and trying not to make the best of things," he continued, "it would be more sensible of you to light the fire and make me a cup of tea. Here's plenty of wood, and here's a fireplace large enough to burn a ton of coals a day. I must see to that. Now bustle about a bit; it will do you good. I am always telling you that you ought to be more energetic and active."

" Is there no servant in the house ? " she asked, wearily. She had taken off her mantle, and having wrapped her child in it and laid her down, was endeavouring to obey her husband's orders. " You said you had one."

" So I have, a man-servant. I engaged him expressly for you."

" The boy at the gate ? "

" Yes ; and here he is, loaded. That's right, Tom ; be sharp and willing, and you'll die a rich man."

Tom Barley was sharp enough to perceive that Mrs. Farebrother was too weak for the work she was endeavouring to perform, and willing enough to step to her assistance.

" May I light the fire ? " he asked, timidly.

She nodded, and sinking into a chair, lifted her child from the floor and nursed her. Seeing her thus engaged, and Tom busy on his knees, Miser Farebrother ran out, and he and the driver between them carried in the rest of the things, the most important being the miser's desk, which he had conveyed at once to the bedroom above. His mind was easier when he saw that precious depository in a place of safety.

Meanwhile Tom Barley was proving himself a most cheerful and capable servant.

"When his honour told me," he whispered, "that he was coming here late at night with you and the baby—a little girl, ain't it?—I thought it would be chilly without a fire, so I cleaned out the fireplace and the chimbley, and got a lot of wood together. There's plenty of it—enough to last a lifetime. Don't you move, now; I can make tea. Used to make mother's. Where's the things? In the basket? Yes; here they are. Here's the kittle, and here's the tea, in a bloo' paper; and here's the teapot; and here's two cups; and here's a bottle of milk and some sugar. It's a blazing fire—ain't it? That's the best of dry wood. The kittle 'll bile in a minute—it's biling already!"

From time to time the delicate woman gave him a grateful look, which more than repaid him, and caused him to double his exertions to make her comfortable. By the time the tea was made, Miser Farebrother had completed the removal of the goods, and had settled with the driver, after a good deal of grumbling at the extortionate demand.

" You can go, Tom," he said to the lad. " Be up early in the morning and make the fire."

"Good-night, your honour."

"Did you hear me tell you to go?" exclaimed Miser Farebrother.

Tom Barley received a kind look from Mrs. Farebrother as he left the room, and he went away perfectly happy.

In another hour the house was quiet and the light extinguished. Miser Farebrother was in secure possession of Parksides, and he fell asleep in the midst of a calculation of how much money he would save in rent in the course of the next twenty years. Other calculations also ran through his head in the midst of his fitful slumbers—calculations of figures and money, and interest, and sharp bargains with needy men, clients he was bleeding to his own profit. No thought in which figures and money did not find a place did he bestow upon the more human aspect of his life, in which there was to be almost immediately an important change.

3—2

Within a fortnight of her entrance into the desolate house Mrs. Farebrother lay upon her death-bed. She had been weak and ailing for months past, and the night's journey from London, no less than the deep unhappiness which, since her marriage, had drawn the roses from her cheeks and made her heart heavy and sad, now hastened her end. As she lay upon the ancient stately bed from which she was never to rise, a terrible loneliness fell upon her. Her darling child was by her side, mercifully asleep; her husband was moving about the apartment; the sunbeams falling through the window brought no comfort to the weary heart — all was so desolate, so desolate! In a trembling voice she called her husband to her.

"Well?" he asked.

"I must see my sister," she said.

"I will not have her," he cried. "You are well enough without her. I will not have her here!"

"I am well enough—to die!" she murmured. "I must see my sister before I go."

"You are frightening yourself unnecessarily," said Miser

Farebrother, fretfully. "You are always full of fancies, and putting me to expense. You never had the slightest consideration for me—not the slightest. You think of nobody but yourself."

"I am frightened of this place," she found strength to say. "I cannot, I will not, die here alone! I must see my sister, I must see my sister!"

Still he made no movement to comply with her request.

"If you do not send for her at once," said his wife, "I will get up and go from the house and die in the roadway. God will give me strength to do it. I must see my sister, I must see my sister!"

Awed, if not convinced, and fearful, too, lest any disturbance which it was in his power to avoid might bring him into unfavourable notice, and interfere with his cherished plans, he said, reluctantly, "I will send for her."

"You are not deceiving me? You are not promising what you do not intend to perform?"

"I will send for her, I tell you."

"If you do not," she said—and there was a firmness in her weak tones which was not without its effect upon him—

"misfortune will attend you all the days of your life. Nothing you do will prosper."

He was superstitious, and believed in omens; and this sounded like a prophecy, the warning of which he dared not neglect. His wife's eyes followed him as he stepped to his desk and sat down and wrote. Presently he left the room, and went in search of Tom Barley, to whom he gave a letter, bidding him to post it in the village. Grumbling at what he had done, he returned to his wife.

"Is my sister coming?" she asked.

"I have written to her," he replied. "Go to sleep and rest. You will be better in the morning."

"Yes," she sighed, as she pressed her child close to her bosom, "I shall be better in the morning. Oh, my sweet flower! my heart's treasure! Guard her, gracious Lord! Make her life bright and happy—as mine once promised to be! I could have given love for love; but it was denied to me. Not mine the fault—not mine, not mine!"

The day waned, the evening shadows fell, and night came on. Upon a table at some distance from the bed was one thin tallow candle, the feeble flame of which flickered dismally. During the long weary hours Mrs. Farebrother did not sleep; she dozed occasionally; but the slightest sound aroused her. In her light slumbers she dreamt of incidents in her happy girlhood before she was married—incidents apparently trivial, but not really so because of the sweet evidences of affection which made them memorable: a song, a dance, a visit to the sea-side, a ramble in fragrant woods; innocent enjoyments from which sprang fond imaginings never to be realized. Betweenwhiles, when she was awake, the gloom of the room and the monstrous shadows thrown by the dim light upon portions of the walls and ceilings distressed her terribly, and she needed all her strength of mind to battle against them. In these transitions of sensation were expressed all the harmonies and discordances of mortal life. Bitter to her had been their fruit!

An hour before midnight she heard the sound of carriage wheels without, and she sat straight up in her bed from excitement, and then fell back exhausted.

"It is my sister," she said, faintly, to her husband. "Let her come up at once. Thank God, she is here in time!"

Her sister bent fondly and in great grief over her. Between these two existed a firm and faithful affection, but the circumstances of Mrs. Farebrother's marriage had caused them to see very little of each other of late years.

"Attend to my darling Phœbe," whispered Mrs. Farebrother; "there is no female servant in the house. Oh, I am so glad you have come before it was too late !"

"Do not say too late, my dearest," said her sister ; but her heart was faint within her as she gazed upon the pallid face and the thin wasted hands ; "there are happy years before you."

"Not one, not one !" murmured Mrs. Farebrother.

"Why did you not send for me before ? "

The dying woman made no reply, and her sister undressed little Phœbe, and placed her in a cot by the mother's bedside. Then she smoothed the sheets and pillows, and sat quietly, with her sister's hand in hers.

"It is like old times," murmured Mrs. Farebrother, wistfully. "You were always good to me. Tell me, my dear—put your head close to mine—oh, how sweet, how sweet !

Were it not for my darling child I should think that Heaven was shining upon me ! "

" What is it you want to know, dear ? You were about to ask me something."

" Yes, yes. Tell me—are you happy at home ? "

" Very happy."

" Truly and indeed ? "

" Truly and indeed. We are not rich, but that does not matter."

" Your husband is good to you ? "

" There is no one in the world like him ; he is the best, the noblest, the most unselfish of men ! " But here, with a sudden feeling of remorse, she stopped. The contrast between her bright home and the gloomy home of her sister struck her with painful force ; to speak of the joys of the one seemed to accentuate the miseries of the other.

" Go on, dear," said Mrs. Farebrother, gently ; "it does not hurt me, indeed it does not ; I have grown so used, in other homes, to what you see around you here that custom has made it less bitter than it once was. It makes me happy to hear of your happiness, and it holds out a glad prospect that my dear child, when she grows up, may have a little share in it."

"She shall, she shall; I promise it solemnly."

"Thank you, dear. So you must go on telling me of your good husband. He is still in his bank?"

"Yes, dear; and hopes for a rise before long. He is always full of hope, and that is worth a great deal—it means so much! He thinks of nothing but his home, and those in it. He dotes upon the children."

"The dear children! Are they well and strong?"

"Yes, dear; and they grow prettier and prettier every day."

" You must kiss them fondly for me, and give them my dear love."

" I will be sure to. You must not talk any more just now; you are tired out. Try and sleep."

"I think I shall be able. God bless you, dear!"

" God bless you, dearest!"

In a few moments, the tension of anxious watching and waiting being over, Mrs. Farebrother slept. Her sister gazed at her solicitously and mournfully. At such a time the cherished memories of old are burdened with a sadness which weighs heavily upon the heart.

"She is not so ill as she fancies, is she ?"

It was Miser Farebrother who spoke to her. She rose softly, and led him from the bed, so that their conversation should not disturb the sufferer.

"Why did you not send me a telegram instead of a letter ?"

"A telegram !" he cried. "Do you think I am made of money ?"

"I am not thinking of your money : I am thinking of my sister. What does the doctor say ? "

"The doctor !" he exclaimed. "I have none."

Gentle-natured as she was, she looked at him in horror.

"You have none—and my sister dying !"

"It is not true," he whined, thinking of the inconvenience such an event would cause him ; "it cannot be true. She was well a few days ago. I cannot afford doctors. You are all in a conspiracy to rob me !"

"I was told as I came along that this great house is yours."

. " Yes, it is—my property, my own."

" And a great deal of land around, and everything in the place."

" Yes, it is—all mine, all mine !" And then, with a sudden suspicion, " Do you intend to dispute it ? "

" Heaven forbid ! What is it to do with me—except that when you speak of ruin to me, and of not being able to afford a doctor, you are speaking what is false. Why did you marry ? "

" I don't know," he replied, wringing his hands, " I don't know. I ought never to have done it. I ought to have lived alone, with nobody to keep but myself."

" It would have been better for my poor sister. But she is your wife, and I shall not allow her to suffer as she is suffering without seeking medical assistance. I have never been in this neighbourhood, and know nothing about it. Where is the nearest doctor ? "

" I can't tell you ; I am almost as much a stranger here as you are."

" There must be one not very far off. Who was the lad who opened the door for me when I came to-night ? "

" My servant, Tom Barley. What do you want him for ? He is asleep by this time. He has work to do the first thing in the morning."

"Where does he sleep ? "

" Outside; in the stable."

" I shall find it. You must write a few words on paper for me."

" I'll do nothing of the sort. You shan't force me to put my name to anything. Do you think I am not up to such tricks ? "

" If you don't do as I say I will bring a lawyer here as well as a doctor."

This woman possessed a sweet and gentle nature, and nothing but the evidence of an overwhelming wrong could have so stirred it to sternness. Miser Farebrother was terrified at the threat of bringing a lawyer into the house; and as he had given way to his wife earlier in the day, so now was he compelled by his fears to give way to her sister. He wrote as she directed :

" Mr. Farebrother, of Parksides, urgently requests the

doctor to come immediately to his house to see Mrs. Fare-brother, who, he fears, is seriously ill."

He fought against two words—"urgently," because it might cause the doctor to make a heavier charge; and "seriously," because a construction that he had been neglectful might be placed on it. But his sister-in-law was firm, and he wrote as she dictated.

"I will send the lad with it," said Miser Farebrother.

"I will send him myself," said his sister-in-law. "There must not be a moment's delay."

There was no need for her to seek Tom Barley in the stable; he was sitting up in the kitchen below.

She gave him the letter, and desired him to run as fast as he could to the village and find a doctor, who was to come back with him. If the doctor demurred, and wanted to put it off till the following day, he was to be told that it was a matter of life and death.

Tom Barley was visibly disturbed when he heard this.

"Who is it, lady?" he asked. "His honour's wife, or the baby?"

"His wife. You're a kind-hearted lad, and won't waste a moment, will you?"

"No, lady; trust me."

He was not above taking the sixpence she offered him, and he ran out of the house like a shot.

Within the hour he was back with the doctor, whose looks were grave as he examined his patient.

"There is hope, doctor?" said Mrs. Farebrother's sister. "Tell me there is hope!"

He shook his head, and gently told her she must prepare for the worst.

"She is past prescribing for," he said. "I can do nothing for her. She has been for some time in a decline."

The sentence being passed, she had no room in her heart for any other feeling than pity for her dying sister. In the sunrise, when the sweet air was infusing strength into fresh young life, the end came. Mrs. Farebrother whispered to her sister that she wished to speak to her husband alone. Thoroughly awed, he sat by her side. She made no reference to the past; she uttered no reproaches. She spoke only of their child, and begged him to be good to her.   He promised all that she asked of him.

"You will get some good woman into the house to take care of her?" she said.

"Yes; I promise."

"And my sister must see her whenever she wishes to do so."

"Yes."

"And when our dear one is old enough and strong enough you will let her go to my sister, and stop with her a little now and then?   It will do her good to mix with children of her own age."

"Yes; I promise."

"As you deal by her, so will you be dealt by.   May Heaven prosper you in all worthy undertakings!   Kiss me. Let there be peace and forgiveness between us."

He kissed her, and sat a little apart while she and her sister, their cheeks nestling, exchanged their last words.

"Look after my treasure," whispered the mother.

"I will, dear, as tenderly and carefully as if she were one of my own."

" You must come here and see her sometimes; he has promised that you may ; and when she grows up you will let her come to you ? "

"She will always be lovingly welcome. My home is hers if she should ever need one."

"God bless you! May your life be prosperous and ever happy ! "

Before noon she drew her last breath, and Parksides was without a mistress.

CHAPTER IV

PHŒBE AND THE ANGELS.

IT did not long remain so.   In less than a fortnight after Mrs. Farebrother's death a housekeeper was installed in Parksides.   Her name was Mrs. Pamflett, and her age thirty.   Being called "Mrs.," the natural inference was that she was either wife or widow; but as no questions were put to her on this point there were none to answer, and it certainly did not appear to be anybody's business but her own.   Miser Farebrother, being entirely wrapped up in his money-bags, gave the entire household into the care of Mrs. Pamflett, one of its items being the motherless child Phœbe.   A capable housekeeper, thrifty, careful, and willing to work, Miser Farebrother was quite satisfied with her performance of her duties ; but she was utterly unfit to rear a child so young as Phœbe, for whom, it must be confessed, she had no particular love, and Phœbe would have fared badly in many ways had it not been for her aunt.

Mrs. Lethbridge lived in London, in the not very aristocratic neighbourhood of Camden Town. She and Phœbe's mother had been married on the same day—one to a man whose miserly habits were unknown, and had, indeed, not at that time grown into a confirmed disease; the other to a bank clerk, who was expected to keep up the appearance of a gentleman, and fitly rear and educate a family, upon a salary of a hundred and eighty pounds a year. Fortunately for him and his wife, their family was not numerous, consisting of one son and one daughter. With Miser Farebrother they had nothing in common; he so clearly and unmistakably discouraged their attempts to cement an affectionate or even a friendly intimacy that they had gradually and surely dropped away from each other. This was a great grief to the sisters, but the edict issued by Miser Farebrother was not to be disputed.

"I will not allow your sister or her husband to come to the house," he had said to his wife when, in the early days of their married life, she remonstrated with him; later on she had not the courage or the spirit to expostulate against his harsh decrees, to which she submitted with a breaking

4—2

heart. "They are a couple of busybodies, and you can tell them so if you please, with my compliments."

Mrs. Farebrother did not tell her sister what her husband called them, but she wrote and said that for the sake of peace they had better not come to see her. The Lethbridges mournfully acquiesced; indeed, they had no alternative: they could not force themselves into the house of a man who would not receive them.

"But if we can't go to her," said Mrs. Lethbridge, "Laura"—which was Mrs. Farebrother's Christian name— "can come to us."

This, also, after a little while, Miser Farebrother would not allow.

"I will not," he said, "have my affairs talked about by people who are not friendly to me."

"That is your fancy," said Mrs. Farebrother; "they would be very happy if you would allow them to be friendly."

"Of course," he sneered, "so that they could poke their heads into my business. I tell you I will not have it."

She sighed, and submitted; and thereafter, when she and her sister met, it was by appointment in a strange place.

Even these rare meetings, upon their being discovered, were prohibited, and thus Miser Farebrother succeeded in parting two sisters who loved each other devotedly.

" Whatever Laura saw in that miserly bear," said Mrs. Lethbridge, indignantly, to her husband, "to marry him is a mystery I shall never be able to discover."

But this mystery is of a nature common enough in the matrimonial market, and may be attributed to thousands of ill-assorted couples.

It was plainly Miser Farebrother's intention to discourage Mrs. Lethbridge's visits to Parksides after the death of his wife; promises were in no sense sacred to him, even death-bed promises, unless their performance was necessary to his interests, and in this instance he very soon decided that it was not.

" You perceive," he said to Mrs. Lethbridge, "that I have a housekeeper to look after the child. You are giving yourself a deal of unnecessary trouble trudging down here —for what ? To ascertain whether she is properly dressed ? You see she is. . Whether she has enough to eat ? She looks well enough, doesn't she ? Don't you think you had

better devote yourself to your own domestic affairs instead
of prying into mine? Your husband must be very rich that
you can afford to pay railway fares and cab fares to come to
a house where you are not wanted."

This, in effect, was the sum of his efforts to prevent
her from visiting Parksides; and his sneers and slighting
allusions, made from time to time, were successful in cur-
tailing her visits to his house during the young childhood
of little Phœbe. They were not successful, however, in
putting a stop to them altogether, until Phœbe was fourteen
years of age, from which time her intercourse with her relatives was maintained by the young girl's visits to Camden
Town—happy visits, lasting seldom less than two or three
days. Until Phœbe was fourteen, her aunt came down to
Parksides only once in every three months. Occasionally
Mrs. Lethbridge caught a glimpse of Miser Farebrother,
whose welcome, if he gave her one at all, was of the surliest;
and as between her and Mrs. Pamflett a strong and silent
antipathy had been contracted from their first interview,
Mrs. Lethbridge's visits could not be said to be of the pleasantest. But for the sake of her dead sister, whom she had

so fondly loved, and of the motherless child, whose sweet ways endeared her to the good aunt, she bore with all the slights that were put upon her; and although she spoke of them at home to her husband, she never mentioned them to her children.

From two to fourteen years of age, Phœbe may be said to have grown up almost in loneliness. Her father rarely noticed her, and Mrs. Pamflett, a peculiar, strange, and silent woman, evinced no desire for her society. The child's nature was sweet and susceptible enough to have given an ample return for proffered affection, and, although she was not at the time aware of it (such speculations being too profound for her young mind), she had great cause for gratitude that her life was not entirely deprived of it. It has unhappily often happened that sweet waters have been turned bitter by unsympathetic contact, and this might have been the case with our Phœbe, had it not been for Mrs. Lethbridge and Tom Barley. Mrs. Lethbridge had made herself so loved by her niece that her visits came to be eagerly looked forward to by the girl, and to be all the more enjoyed because they were rare. Her love for the child was manifested as much, if not more, in her absence than in her presence. When Phœbe could read or spell through written hand, Mrs. Lethbridge wrote letters to her, to which the child replied. Phœbe's letters were slipped unstamped in the post-office by Tom Barley, and for a long time she was not aware of the unfair expense to which her aunt was being put, and for which Miser Farebrother alone was responsible. Mrs. Lethbridge never mentioned it to her niece. Then there were the books which Mrs. Lethbridge brought or sent—a source of so much delight and exquisite enjoyment that the remembrance of those youthful days was with Phœbe a sweet remembrance through all her life.

Living in a certain sense alone in a great mansion, it is not to be wondered at that a current of romance was formed in the young girl's nature. Neglected and uncared for as she was by those immediately about her, there was no restriction upon her movements through the old house. Certain rooms were prohibited to her, Mrs. Pamflett's room and her father's bedroom, which served also as an office. To this latter apartment, when she passed fourteen years of age, Phœbe was sometimes called—otherwise she was forbidden to enter it. With these exceptions she was free to wander whither she would, and she would often pass hours together in a room never occupied by the household, and which had an irresistible fascination for her. It was of octagonal shape, and there were faded paintings on the walls and rotting tapestries. Originally it was most likely used as a library, for it contained book-cases and large pieces of furniture, a table, two secretaries, and a huge chair, so heavy that Phœbe could not even move it. The carvings about the room and upon the furniture were strangely grotesque— fantastic heads and faces, animals such as were never seen in nature, and uncouth forms of men which had no existence save in the feverish imaginations of the designers. These contorted shapes and grotesque faces might have been supposed to be sufficiently repulsive to cause a sensitive child to avoid them, but in truth they were in themselves an attraction to Phœbe, who discovered no terrors in them to affright her. There was, however, in the room an attraction of a more congenial kind, in which grace, harmony, proportion, and a most exquisite beauty were conspicuous.

High up in a corner, opposite a window which faced the west, was a carving of angels' heads, hanging over, as it were, and looking down upon the spectator. Devoid of natural colour as they were, so grand and wondrous had been the skill of the carver that it was as though a multitude of joyous, rosy-cheeked children were bending down to obtain a view of a scene as delightful as they themselves presented. The lips smiled, the eyes sparkled, the faces beamed with life. This marvel, cut out of brown wood, was, indeed, something more than the perfection of art and grace—it was an enchantment which made the heart glad to behold. And in the evening, when the effulgent radiances of a glorious sunset shone upon the wonder and played about it, touching the dainty faces with alluring light, it filled even the soul of our young child with a holy joy.

This was Phœbe's favourite room ; and here she would sit and read, and sometimes stand, with folded hands, looking upward at the enchanting group, with the sunset's colours upon them ; and in her eyes would dwell a rapture which made her as lovely as the fairest of the faces she gazed upon. Thus she grew up to a graceful and beautiful womanhood, encompassed by sweet and grand imaginings which purified her soul.

CHAPTER V.

LONG before this, Tom Barley had grown to manhood's estate: the only estate of which he was owner and was ever likely to possess. But, although he had no landed property of his own to look after, he had an object in life. He conceived it to be his particular privilege to protect Phœbe, to run of her errands, and to be in a general way her willing and cheerful slave. Had he been able to intelligently and logically express himself upon the point in the early years of his connection with Miser Farebrother, it would have been ascertained that he founded his position upon the facts that he had held Phœbe in his arms upon her first introduction to Parksides, that he had been smiled upon by her mother, that he had attended the poor lady's funeral as an important and very genuine mourner, and that, besides, he was in the service of Miser Farebrother, who had promised to make his fortune. Later on, these unexpressed motives were merged into an absorbing devotion for the young girl, for whom he grew to entertain a kind of worship which removed her from his estimate of the ordinary mortal. A rough-and-ready knight he, ready to sacrifice himself at any moment for the queen of his idolatry. She, it must be confessed, received his homage very willingly, and as though it were rightly her due, and, unconsciously to herself, she richly repaid him for his services : by allowing him to initiate her into woodland wonders with which he had made himself familiar, by constant smiles and bright looks, by accepting the assistance of his hands when she crossed tumble-down stiles, and in a hundred other general ways of faith and belief in him which were a finer reward to Tom Barley than money could have been. Of this latter commodity he had little enough. The twopence a week which Miser Farebrother paid him was all he ever received from his employer, in addition to scraps of food from the kitchen upon which he managed to subsist. But, living in civilized society, clothing was a prescribed necessity, and was not to be obtained upon eight-and-eightpence a year. Tom dropped a hint or two, but Miser Farebrother was oblivious, and callous to the peeping of flesh through tatters.

"You extravagant dog," he said, "I did not undertake to clothe you. Look at me : *I* can't afford fine new clothes! Go and hang about the village, when you've nothing to do here, and look for an odd job. That's the way to earn honest pennies. Many a millionaire began with less. And, Tom," he added, "when you've saved a few shillings, I dare say I can find an old pair of trousers that I'll sell you cheap."

Tom profited by the suggestion, and in a little while found the way to earn a good many honest pennies. Miser Farebrother fished out of his scanty wardrobe some tattered garments, which he disposed of to Tom, and it was then that the lad exhibited himself in a new character, which drove the miser to desperation. He bargained with his master and beat him down to the last penny; Tom was not devoid of shrewdness, and he was beginning to understand the miser.

"If every man was as generous as I am," grumbled Miser

Farebrother, at the conclusion of their first barter, "he'd soon be on the road to ruin."

"They're full of holes," said Tom, turning the clothes over and examining them ruefully. The miser would not allow him to handle them until the bargain was completed and the money safe in his pocket: "look here, and here!"

"Look here, and here, you dog!" retorted Miser Farebrother. "Do I charge you anything for their being too big for you? Can't you cut off the bottoms of the trousers, and patch the knees with the extra bits? You ought to give the pieces back to me; but I make you a present of them."

Tom was quick enough at taking a hint. Being thrown upon his own resources, and imbued with the cheerfulest of spirits, he soon became proficient with the needle, and, by patching here and darning there, managed to maintain a tolerably decent appearance. He might have done better, had he not been afflicted by an insatiable hungering for brandy-balls, which, at three a penny, was a temptation not to be resisted whenever he had a copper to spare. To see him rolling one in his mouth was a picture of unalloyed bliss.

Mrs. Pamflett and he were not good friends, and an incident which will be presently related did not dispose them more favourably to each other. He was more fortunate with Mrs. Lethbridge. This good-hearted woman had noticed his unselfish devotion to Phœbe, and he won her favour thereby. Many a small silver bit found its way from her pocket to his; and more than once she bore with her to Parksides a little parcel containing a waistcoat, or an under-shirt, or a couple of pairs of socks, which had served their time at home, but which were not so utterly worn out as not to be useful to Tom. He was very grateful for these gifts, and showed his appreciation of them by forcing a brandy-ball upon her now and then. She went further. Impressed by Phœbe's constant praise of the young fellow, and recognizing that the girl had near her, when she was absent, a stanch and faithful champion, ever ready to protect and defend her, she took Tom Barley into her confidence.

" Can you read, Tom ? " she asked.

"Yes, lady," he replied. "Square letters—not round uns. And I can write 'em."

Thereupon Mrs. Lethbridge wrote her name and address in Camden Town on a piece of paper, in square letters; and Tom spelt them aloud.

"Keep this by you," said Mrs. Lethbridge; "and if ever anything happens to Miss Farebrother, and you don't know what to do, come for me at once. Here's a two-shilling piece. You must not spend it; you must put it carefully away, in case you need it for this special purpose. The railway fare to London and back is eighteenpence; an omnibus will bring you very near to my house for threepence. You understand?"

"I understand, lady. But trust me for taking care of Miss Phœbe."

"I do, Tom; but something we don't think of just now might happen, and Miss Phœbe might want you to come for me. Or you might think, 'I wish Miss Phœbe had somebody with her who feels like a mother to her, and who loves her very tenderly.'"

"So do I, lady," said Tom, in an earnest tone. "I'll do as you tell me. You can trust me."

"I know it, Tom, and so does Miss Phœbe. She says she doesn't know what she should do without you."

"*I* shouldn't know what to do without *her*," said Tom, feeling very proud. That he was trusted, and that his young mistress valued his services, gave him a feeling of self-respect.

From that day he became more than ever Phœbe's faithful knight, and it was when Phœbe was twelve years of age that the incident occurred, springing out of his championship of the little maid, which increased Mrs. Pamflett's aversion to him. Tom at that time was twenty-four, and had grown into a long lean man, looking two or three inches taller than he really was because of his extreme lankiness. His coats and trousers were now always too short for his arms and legs, and he was remarkable for a lavish protuberance and exhibition of bone. He was very strong, and was noted as a fleet runner; he could start off at a rapid swinging gait, and keep his wind and pace for hours. This accomplishment had brought grist to his mill

MRS. PAMFLETT RECOMMENDS A NEW CLERK.   67

on several occasions, when he was backed by a sporting publican against men who had an opinion of themselves as fast runners. "Five shillings if you win, Tom," said the sporting publican, "and nothing if you lose." This was a sufficient incentive, and Tom invariably won, to the satisfaction of most of the on-lookers, for he was a favourite with all who knew him. He had weaknesses, but no vices; his taste for brandy-balls rather increased than diminished with his years, and though temptations to drink were frequently thrown out to him, he was never known to touch a glass of liquor. Not at all a bad sort of fellow, this Tom Barley, and a very handy man to look after our little heroine.

One of his weaknesses was a fondness for all kinds of street shows, most especially for "Punch and Judy," at which he would stand and gaze and laugh with the heartiness of a boy. A capital ladder was he for small children, whom he would hoist to his shoulders in order that they might have a good view of the show, and his kindly nature would always gravitate to the weakest and smallest of the eager throng. It was during a representation of this immortal tragical comedy that a new acquaintance was made by Tom Barley and his young mistress. The meeting became historical, by force of exciting detail and vivid colour, and one small boy was covered with glory. It is opportunity that creates heroes.

To commence at the commencement, it was on this day revealed to Phœbe and Tom that Mrs. Pamflett had a son. She had never spoken of him to them, and when he made his first appearance at Parksides they were absent in the village. His mission at Parksides was the opening of a career.

Miser Farebrother had an office in London, in which he transacted the greater portion of his business. It was his habit to go to London every morning and return every evening. He had a third-class annual ticket, every fresh renewal of which drove daggers into his heart. A clerk who had starved in his employment had suddenly taken courage and left him, impressed by the idea that he could starve more agreeably in another situation; for Miser Farebrother not only paid the smallest of wages, but he was a bully and a tyrant to those who were dependent upon him.

On the evening before the day on which the historical events about to be recorded took place a violent altercation had occurred between Miser Farebrother and his slave of a clerk, and the man, suddenly jumping from his stool, flung down his pen, took his hat from the peg, damned Miser Farebrother, and left the office, to which he swore he would never return. Miser Farebrother was very much astonished; the man had been useful and had grown into his ways, and he had so browbeaten and oppressed him that he did not think a particle of spirit was left in the drudge. And all at once, here he was in a state of rebellion !

" You'll die in a ditch ! " he called after the man.

There were crumbs of comfort, however, in the act which caused Miser Farebrother to rub his hands with satisfaction. His clerk had left on a Thursday : four days' wages saved.

There were confidences between the miser and Mrs. Pamflett, and when he returned to Parksides he related to her what had occurred.

" You will want a new clerk," she said. " Take Jeremiah."

Miser Farebrother put his right hand up to his chin, and repeated, musingly, " Take Jeremiah."

" You couldn't do better," said Mrs. Pamflett, "and you are almost certain to do worse."

She spoke in a hard tone ; there was no pleading in her voice and manner : had there been, the probability is that she would not have succeeded.

" How old is he now ? " asked Miser Farebrother.

" Seventeen last birthday."

" Decent looking ? "

" Yes."　　　　　　　'

" A good writer ? "

" Here is his last letter to me," said Mrs. Pamflett, hand-ing it to the miser.

He examined it carefully ; the writing was excellent. He returned it to his housekeeper.

" How about his figures ? "

" He is splendid at them. That is what he was dis-tinguished for at school."

" Was he distinguished for anything else ? For instance, for keeping his own counsel ? "

" He can do that."

" Is he fond of pleasure ? "

" He wants to get along in the world."

" Willing to work hard ? "

" Try him."

" I will think of it," said Miser Farebrother, going to his room. It was not his habit to do things in a hurry.

He passed the night as usual writing in his account-books, and making calculations of money and dates, and reckoning up compound interest at different rates of percentage per month. He never lent money at interest per annum, but always at compound interest per month, a system which swelled his profits enormously. A ledger slipped from the table to the ground, and stooping to reach it, he found himself unable to rise. He beat the floor with his hands, and called out for his housekeeper; but it was many minutes before she heard him and came to his help. She assisted him to his feet, and into his chair, where he sat, twisting and groaning.

" Rub my back, rub my back ! Lower, lower ! A little more to the left ! No; that's not the place ! Ah, now

you're right.   Keep   rubbing — harder,   harder.   Oh !
oh ! "

" I told you the other night," said Mrs. Pamflett, composedly, as she carried out his instructions, "when you
walked home from the station in the sopping rain, that
you'd catch lumbago ; and now you've got it."

" Oh ! oh !" cried Miser Farebrother.   " You're a witch,
you're a witch !   You laid a spell upon me.   What did you
do it for ?   Do you think I shall put you down in my will,
and that my death will make you rich ?   You're mistaken ;
I've no money to leave and if I had, *you* shouldn't have it.
No one should have it—no one.   ' Walk home in the rain !'
—what else could I do ?   Can I afford carriages to ride in ?
You know I can't ; you know it, you know it !   Rub away
—harder—harder !   Have you got no life in you ? "

He lay back in his chair, gasping, his pains somewhat
relieved.

" You won't be able to move to-morrow," said Mrs. Pamflett ; "and now you've begun to have lumbago, it will
never leave you."

" What !   You're putting more spells on me, are you ?

Witches ought to be burnt. It's a good job there's nothing particular to do at the office to-morrow; only it isn't safe to leave it alone day or night."

"No, it isn't," said Mrs. Pamflett. "Somebody ought to sleep there. I always thought that. Jeremiah could. You'd best get to bed now; I'll help you. Then I'll get some turpentine and flannel; it will do you good, perhaps. Yes, some person in whom you have confidence, should sleep in the office."

"There's no such person," he snarled. "Everybody tries to rob me—everybody—everybody!"

"How will it be," said Mrs. Pamflett, not in the slightest way ruffled, "when you're laid up a week at a time, and can't go to London to attend your customers? It will happen; I know what lumbago is. Once get it into your bones, there's no driving it out."

"It isn't in my bones; it's only a slight attack. I can walk now if I please. See; I can stand up straight, and— Oh! oh!"

Down he fell again, and when Mrs. Pamflett attempted to assist him he screamed out, "Let me be! let me be!" You're twisting me wrong! You want to kill me!"

Presently, when there was less need for his comical physical contortions, which did not elicit from Mrs. Pamflett either a smile or the slightest expression of sympathy, she returned to the attack.

"Jeremiah is the very person you want. If you don't have him, I shall obtain another situation for him, and then you will lose a treasure."

"A treasure!" he retorted, scornfully. "Of course: every cock crows on its own dunghill. Jeremiah's a precious stone, eh? A very precious stone!"

"He is. He's the brightest, cleverest lad *you've* ever come across."

"Ah," he said, with a cunning cock of his head; "but we don't want 'm too clever; do we?"

"He will do everything you want done in the way you wish," said Mrs. Pamflett, calmly; "and if that doesn't content you, nothing will. He writes well, as you have seen; he knows all about book-keeping; and he's as sharp as a needle."

"Takes after his mother" observed Miser Farebrother, with a sardonic leer.

"No; I was never very clever, I've missed things. He won't, being a man. I'm glad I didn't have a girl. As a rule, I hate them."

"How about Phœbe?"

"She's well enough, but there's not much love lost between us. She don't take to me, and I don't take to her. It's on her side, mostly, not mine. She has nothing to complain of, any more than you have."

"Oh, I don't complain," he said, his wary eyes on her.

"Perhaps it s as well you don't. You must have somebody here, and you would most likely get some one in my place who'd eat you out of house and home. Female servants are a nice set! Shall I send for Jeremiah? Will you see him here to-morrow?"

"Yes," said Miser Farebrother; he was now in bed, and Mrs. Pamflett was tucking him in; "you may send for him. I will see him to-morrow."

CHAPTER VI.

A VERY SMALL BOY COVERS HIMSELF WITH GLORY.

JEREMIAH PAMFLETT presented himself at Parksides at noon. His mother was waiting for him at the gates. A pale, self-possessed woman, upon whose face, to the ordinary observer, was never seen a sign of joy or sorrow, in whose eyes never shone that light of sympathy which draws heart to heart, she became transformed the moment her son appeared. She ran toward him; she pressed him in her arms; she kissed him again and again.

"My boy! my boy!" she murmured.

"Mother," said Jeremiah, "you're rumpling my collar, and you wrote to me to make myself nice."

"And you do look nice, my pet," said Mrs. Pamflett, taking off his shiny belltopper, and blowing away a speck of dust. "How much did you give for this new hat?"

"Six-and-six, in Drury Lane. Don't press your hand

over it like that; you're rubbing the dust into it. I gave
fifteenpence for the necktie and tenpence for this white
handkerchief, and two-and-nine for the shirt. Then there's
the boots and socks and a new walking-stick. And I had
to get shaved."

"Did you, Jeremiah, did you!" exclaimed the proud
mother, passing her hand over his remarkably smooth chin,
guiltless as yet of the remotest indication of hair. "My
boy's growing quite a man!"

"Altogether, with my fare down here, I've spent one
pound six, and you only sent me a sovereign. I had to
borrow the six shillings, and I shall have to pay it back the
moment I get to London."

With a nod and a smile Mrs. Pamflett produced her
purse, and handed six shillings to her son, upon receiving
which Jeremiah hugged her, and winked, as it were inwardly to himself, over her shoulder.

"Another shilling, mother, for luck; now don't be mean.
You haven't got any more sons; don't begrudge your only
one!"

The appeal was irresistible, and Jeremiah received

another shilling, which he greeted with a repetition of the hug and the wink.

"And now, mother, what is it all about? What's the little game? I'm going to make my fortune, am I? Well, I'm willing."

Mrs. Pamflett took him into the kitchen and explained. He was to enter Miser Farebrother's service, she said, if the miser approved of him. The miser was in bed upstairs, laid up with lumbago, and Jeremiah was to be very polite and civil, and not to mind if the miser flew out at him.

This caused Jeremiah to exclaim: "Oh, come, mother, I'm not going to be bullied. I wouldn't stand it from a man twice my size!"

Mrs. Pamflett expressed her admiration of his courage, but said he must keep himself in. Miser Fairbrother was "touchy," because he was in such pain. If Jeremiah was engaged, he was to sleep in the office in London, and if he was steady and attentive he might become the sole manager of Miser Farebrother's business in the course of a few years, and—who knows?—perhaps a partner. She said a great deal more than this to her young hopeful, and she made him thoroughly understand how the land lay.

"And now come up with me," she said. " I will show you into his room."

" But, I say," expostulated Jeremiah, looking greedily at the saucepans on the fire, from one of which an appetizing flavour was escaping, "ain't you going to give me anything to eat ? "

"When you come down, Jeremiah," she replied, "I'll have a nice dinner for you. Can't you smell it ? "

The conformation of Jeremiah Pamflett's pug-nose became accentuated by reason of its owner giving half a dozen vigorous sniffs, and having thus tasted the pleasures of hope he followed his mother upstairs to Miser Farebrother's bed-room. The miser was in bed, groaning in his night-cap, and pouring out imprecations upon fate. Mrs. Pamflett assisted him into the easiest posture, and he cocked his eye at Jeremiah, who had suddenly become very humble and subservient. He was the personification of meekness as he stood in the presence of the queer-looking night-capped figure in bed, gazing at him with eyes which seemed to pierce him through and through.

"So this is Jeremiah, is it?" he said.

Mrs. Pamflett smiled a beaming assent.

"Draw that table closer to the bed; now those sheets of paper; now the pen and ink; now the blotting-paper; now a chair for the lad. Go; leave us alone."

The interview lasted an hour, at the end of which Jeremiah presented himself before his anxious mother with a sly look of self-satisfaction. His first words were:

"Oh! but ain't he a scorcher? Cayenne pepper ain't in it with him. Talk of sharpness! Well, I thought I wasn't bad, but he licks Blue Peter. He put me through, I can tell you."

"Are you engaged, Jeremiah?" asked Mrs. Pamflett, her fond hands about his clothes, setting them right. "What questions did he ask you, and how did you answer them? Why don't you speak?"

"Shan't say a blessed word," was the affectionate reply, "till I've had something to eat. Serve up, mother; I'm as empty as a drum."

Mrs. Pamflett obeyed, and set before him a dish of haricot sufficient for a young family. It was a special favourite with him, and he bestowed upon his mother the commendation that she was "a tip-topper, and no flies about it," which afforded her as much pleasure as an exhibition medal would have done. He washed down his copious meal with two glasses of ale, and throwing himself back in his chair, gave her an account of the interview. He had written no end of things at the miser's dictation—letters, threats of what would be done if certain sums of money were not forthcoming at stated times, and statements of conversations which he was supposed to be listening to without the clients being aware of it. Then he was set to calculate sums of great intricacy—to add up, to multiply, not only pounds, shillings and pence, but farthings and fractions of farthings. He performed these tasks to Miser Farebrother's satisfaction. "I'm a regular dab at figures, you know," said Jeremiah to his mother; and the end of it was that he was engaged, and that the miser had promised to make his fortune.

"I mean to make it, mother," said Jeremiah.

" I shall live to see you ride in your carriage," said she.

" I'll be able to afford it one day ; but "—with a touch of shrewdness of which Miser Farebrother himself might have been proud—" it will be cheaper, don't you think, to ride in other people's ? "

This made Mrs. Pamflett laugh, and she kissed him, and praised him for his cleverness. She wished him to remain with her the whole of the day ; but he said he must get back to London, and after screwing two or three more shillings out of her, he bade her good-bye. She stood at the gates watching him till he was out of sight, sucking the knob of his new walking stick, and flourishing it with an air. He was in the mood for enjoyment, and he was not at all in the hurry he expressed to get back to the metropolis. Meeting a small urchin in a lane, he bailed him up.

" What's your name, you scoundrel ? " he said, setting the boy before him.

" Roger," said the trembling lad, whose age might have been six, and was certainly not more.

Jeremiah gave him a violent shaking. " Say ' sir ' ; say ' Roger, sir.' "

"Roger, sir."

" Say it louder. If you cry, I'll chop you into little bits."

" Roger, sir."

"What are you doing here ? "

" Nothing, sir."

" How dare you do nothing ? Bow to me."

The frightened little chap bowed, whipping off his cap at Jeremiah's command.

" Bow three times. Lower—lower—lower ! " The little chap obeyed, bowing almost to the stones.

" Now say, ' I beg your pardon, *sir*; and I'll never do so again.' "

"I beg your pardon, *sir*; and I'll never do so agin."

Jeremiah slapped his face, and walked away, whistling. It was a good commencement. He was really enjoying himself. When he reached the village another excitement greeted him. There was a " Punch and Judy " being shown, and a large crowd, chiefly composed of children, were gathered around the entertainment. Among the on-lookers were Phœbe and Tom Barley. Jeremiah elbowed his way into the centre of the crowd, and presently a girl cried " Oh ! " and

6—2

looked round, rubbing her arm. She was a plain-looking girl, and somebody had given her a sharp pinch. Jeremiah Pamflett looked away, with a successful effort at unconsciousness. Edging a little further on he stationed himself behind another plain girl, who also the next minute cried " Oh ! " and looked round, without discovering her tormentor. This was one of Jeremiah's favourite pastimes, mixing in a crowd of children and pinching the ugly girls. Both Phœbe and Tom Barley were too deeply absorbed in the show to notice these mean diversions, and Jeremiah moved about, enjoying himself to his heart's content, till he found himself standing just behind Phœbe, having pushed between her and Tom. Eyeing her over, to select a nice place for his fingers, he was on the point of operating, when a slight turn on Phœbe's part gave him a view of her face.

" She's too pretty to pinch," thought he ; " I'll kiss her."

Judging his opportunity and the favourable moment, he slyly planted a kiss upon her neck. The young girl started, and blushed all over.

"Tom !" she screamed.

At that precise moment a remarkable incident occurred.

Jeremiah Pamflett felt a strong hand on his collar and another strong hand at his waist, and, presto ! he was twisted off his legs and raised in the air. His next bewildering sensation was being run away with. It was Tom Barley now who was the principal actor. He had observed Jeremiah Pamflett's proceeding, and he had acted on the excitement of the moment, with a vague idea of running away with the delinquent, and administering sound punishment to him by throwing him into a pond if he could find one, or into a prickly hedge, or something of the sort.

There was instant confusion in the crowd. All the children looked after the flying figure of Tom Barley, holding the astonished Jeremiah aloft. The show-men were not entirely dissatisfied, the entertainment being very near its end, and a fair amount of coppers having been already gathered. Toby, an impulsive dog, and somewhat new to the business, could not resist his proclivities, and darted after Tom and Jeremiah. Phœbe, in terror, screamed, " Come back, Tom ! come back ! "

Her voice reached Tom's ears, and he instantly turned back, followed by Toby. Arrived at his starting-point, he dropped Jeremiah to the ground, who slowly rose, in a woeful plight. His nice new clothes were disarranged; buttons were off; there was a rent here and there; he picked up his nice new hat, crushed and out of shape.

"Why don't you hit one of your own size?" he cried, with his right elbow raised to protect his face.

"I haven't hit you yet," said Tom. Phœbe was clinging to his arm. "And now I look at you, I *am* a little too big for you. But you've got to be hit by some one."

"I'll have the law of you!" gasped Jeremiah, gazing ruefully at his hat. "You shall pay for it, or my name ain't Jeremiah Pamflett."

"Oh! Jeremiah Pamflett, is it?" said Tom, in no wise diverted from his intention by the intelligence.

"Come away, Tom," said Phœbe, imploringly. "Let us go home."

If anything could have contributed to Jeremiah's escape, it was this; but Tom Barley's spirit was roused, also his sense of justice, and under such influences he could be firm.

"In a minute or two," he said to her. "There's nothing

to be frightened at. Look here," and he addressed the crowd, "this young London spark has insulted my mistress."

" And he pinched *me !* " exclaimed a girl, light dawning upon her, and through her upon other of Jeremiah's victims.

" He pinched *me !* " " He pinched *me !* " came in a chorus from half a dozen indignant girls.

" That settles it," said Tom. " Is there any one here of his own size, or less, that 'll tackle him for twopence and a brandy-ball ? "

" Couldn't speak fairer," said one of the show-men.

Now among the crowd was a very small boy, several inches below Jeremiah Pamflett in height, but so renowned for his pluck that he had earned the cognomen of " The Bantam."

Forth stepped the Bantam. " I will ! " said he.

" Hooray ! " cried the other boys and girls. " Hooray for the Bantam ! "

" Bray-vo, little un ! " said the show-man.

" Here's your twopence," said Tom Barley, "and your brandy-ball. Fight him."

"Make a ring," said the show-man, delightedly arranging the children in a circle. "I'll see that it's fair play."

Jeremiah and the Bantam were already in the centre, the Bantam with his coat off and his shirt sleeves tucked up. Jeremiah, looking down upon him, inwardly congratulated himself.

"Come on," he said, "and be made a jelly of!"

Nothing daunted, the Bantam squared up, and the battle commenced. It looked "any odds on the long un," the show-man declared, as he inwardly determined to protect the little fellow from too severe a punishment. But a wonder was in store. Despite his size, Jeremiah found it impossible to reach the Bantam, who skipped about in the liveliest fashion, springing up and planting one on Jeremiah's nose, and another on his right eye, and another on his mouth, which puffed up his lips and set all his teeth chattering. In a short time he did not know exactly where he was, and he hit out more wildly. The audience cheered the little champion, and encouraged him by crying, "Go it, Bantam! Go it! Give him another on the nose!" and every now and then "Time!" was called by the show-man, who declared that the Bantam was "a chap after his own heart." At length, Jeremiah Pamflett, completely bewildered, stepping back, tripped and fell flat.

"Any more?" cried the Bantam.

Jeremiah remained on the ground, and did not attempt to rise. The show-man threw up his hat.

"We gives in," he said. "Three cheers for the Bantam!"

They were given with a will; and then a collection was made, and the champion was presented with fourpence half-penny, and, wiping his glory-covered brows, stalked off to the sweet-stuff shop, accompanied by his admirers. Tom and Phœbe took their departure, and the show-men shouldered their Punch and Judy, and walked away with Toby. Jeremiah picked himself up, and crawled to the railway station, shorn of his pride.

CHAPTER VII.

MISER FAREBROTHER ENVIES FAUST.

By the time that Phœbe was eighteen years of age, Jeremiah
Pamflett was firmly established in Miser Farebrother's office
in London. In the miser's shrewd eyes he had justified the
praise his mother had bestowed upon him. A slyer,
smarter manager, Miser Farebrother could scarcely hope
to have. Even the miser himself could not be more ex-
acting with tardy borrowers or more grinding in the collect-
ing of rents ; for Miser Farebrother had now a great many
houses in the poor localities of the metropolis, which, at the
rents for which he let them, paid him a high rate of interest
for his outlay. He had not, in the first instance, purchased
these houses, nor had he ever drifted into the folly of
building one. It was property he had advanced money
upon, which had not been repaid, and as he had calculated
all the chances beforehand, lending at exorbitant interest,
and draining, so to speak, the hearts' blood of his customers,

he made rare bargains in this line. Had he followed his own inclination he would have trusted no man to manage his business; but rheumatism and neuralgic pains were firmly settled in his bones, and frequently for days together he was unable to move out of Parksides. Then Jeremiah Pamflett would come down to him with papers and books, and they would remain closeted together for hours going over the accounts. He had his own private sets of books in Parksides, and he turned Phœbe to account in making them up and in writing for him. This was not a regular, but a fitful employment with the young girl, and her father was satisfied to spare her to go to London, to the house of Aunt Leth in Camden Town, to whom she paid long visits. In that house it may be truly said that Phœbe enjoyed the sunshine of life. Aunt Leth, who taught her own children at home—not caring to send them to school, and not being rich enough to afford a private governess or a tutor for them—taught Phœbe also, and the firmest bonds of love were cemented between them. When Mrs. Lethbridge had married, her house was not at all badly furnished; friends and relatives of her husband had made them many useful household presents, and Mr. Lethbridge had received from his father a special sum to be expended on house furniture. Although but little of a worldly man, Mr. Lethbridge had purchased furniture of a substantial description, and the care taken of it by his good wife made it quite respectable-looking, even after long years of wear and tear. Perhaps the most acceptable of all the wedding presents was a famous piano from a generous uncle, which she cherished and preserved. It was, indeed, to her almost as a living member of her family, and she grew to have a strong affection for it. This will be understood by those who love music as Mrs. Lethbridge did. More and more endeared to them did this treasure become with age, and numberless were the pleasant evenings it afforded them, especially in the spring-time of life, when the hearts of the young people were filled with sweet dreams. By its means they learnt to sing and dance, and poor and struggling as the home of the Lethbridges actually was—evidences of which, mind you, were never seen by others than themselves—there were hours spent in it which richer people might have envied.

Miser Farebrother was content. Phœbe was obtaining an education which did not cost him a shilling, and the meals she ate in her aunt's house were a saving to him. Aunt Leth also was quite a skilful dress-maker, and she made all Phœbe's dresses. A cunning milliner too. Phœbe's hats and bonnets, albeit inexpensive, were marvels of prettiness. All this was worth a deal to Miser Farebrother, who grudged every shilling it cost him to live. He gave nothing to the Lethbridges in return, nor was he asked to give anything. Since Phœbe was fourteen years of age Aunt Leth had not set foot inside the gates of Parksides.

"Let it be well understood," said Miser Farebrother to his daughter, "I am nothing to them, and they are nothing to me. If they expect me to do anything for them, they will be disappointed, and they will have only themselves to blame for it."

"They don't expect you to do anything for them," said Phœbe, with a flush of shame on her face. "They never so much as give it a thought."

"How should they? How should they?" retorted

Miser Farebrother. "It would be so unnatural, wouldn't it? so very unnatural; they being poor, as they say they are, and I being rich as they think I am! They *do* say they're poor, now, don't they?"

"No," said Phœbe, considering; "I never remember their saying so. But they have as much as ever they can do to get along nicely. I know that without being told."

"So have we all, more than ever we can do. *I* can't get along nicely. Everything goes wrong with me—everything; and everybody tries to cheat me. If I wasn't as sharp as a weasel we shouldn't have a roof over our heads. It's the cunning of your aunt and uncle that they don't complain. They say to themselves, 'That old miser, Farebrother'— they *do* call me an 'old miser,' don't they, eh?"—he asked, suddenly, breaking off.

"I never heard them, father."

"But they think it," said Miser Farebrother, looking at Phœbe slyly; "and that's worse—ever so much worse. With people who speak out, you know where you are; it's the quiet cunning ones you have to beware of. They say to themselves, 'That old miser Farebrother will see through us if we complain to his daughter. He'll think we want him to give us some of his money, and that wouldn't please him, he's so fond of it. It will be by far the best to let Phœbe tell him of her own accord, and work upon his feelings in an accidental way, and then perhaps he'll send us a pound or two.' Oh, I know these clever people—I know them well, and can read them through and through! I should like to back them for cunning against some very sharp persons."

"You do them a great injustice, father. They are the dearest people in all the wide world—"

"Of course they are—of course they are," said Miser Farebrother, with a dry laugh. "They have been successful in making you believe it, at all events. That proves their cunning; it's part of their plan."

"It is not," said Phœbe, warmly; "they have no plan of the kind, and as to saying that they have led me on to speak to you about their troubles, and work upon your feelings, you couldn't imagine anything farther from the truth."

"Their troubles, eh!—they let you know they have troubles?"

"If you mean that they wish to get me to talk about them to you, no, father; they haven't let me know in that way. I can see them myself, without being told; and no one can help loving Aunt Leth for her patience and cleverness. Upon my word, it's perfectly wonderful how she manages upon the salary Uncle Leth gets from the bank. Now, father, you *know* that you yourself have led me on to speak of this." (When Phœbe was excited she emphasized a great many words, so that there should be no possibility of her meaning being mistaken.) "*I* didn't commence it; *you* did."

"No, Phœbe; it was you that commenced it."

"How could I, when I never said a word?"

"I saw what was in your mind, Phœbe. You were going to ask me for something for them; it's no use your denying it. I knew it when you shifted about the room, moving things that didn't require moving, and then moving them back again, and keeping on looking at me every now and then when you thought I wasn't looking at you. Oh, I was watching you when you least expected it. I am not easily deceived, and not often mistaken, Phœbe —eh ? "

This was embarrassing, and Phœbe could not help a little laugh escaping her ; for it was a fact that she was watching for a favourable opportunity to ask her father a favour in connection with her relatives. He, observing her furtively from under his brows, perceived that his shot had taken effect, and he waited for Phœbe to continue the conversation, enjoying her discomfiture, and secretly resolving that the Lethbridges should not get a penny from him, not a penny. Phœbe was in hopes that he would assist her out of her dilemma, and throw out a hint upon which she could improve ; but her father did not utter a word, and she was herself compelled to break the silence.

" Well, father, I *was* going to say something about Aunt and Uncle Leth and my cousins."

" I knew you were."

" I have been there a great deal, and they have been very kind to me. If I ever forget their kindness I shall be the most ungrateful girl in the world. Think of the years I have been going to their house, and stopping there, and always being made welcome—"

"Stop a minute, Phœbe," interrupted her father. "'Think of the years!'—yes, yes—you are getting"—and now he regarded her more attentively than he had done for a long time past, and seemed to be surprised at a discovery which forced itself upon him—"You are getting quite a woman—quite a woman!"

"Yes, father," said Phœbe, quietly and modestly; "I shall be eighteen next Saturday. Aunt Leth was saying only last week how like I was to my dear mamma."

Miser Farebrother rose and hobbled across the room and back. It was with difficulty he did this, his bones were so stiff; but when Phœbe stepped forward to assist him, he motioned her angrily away. He accepted, however, the crutch stick which she handed to him; he could not get along without it, but he snatched it from her pettishly. Her mention of her mother disturbed and irritated him. He recalled the few days of her unhappy life at Parksides, and the picture of her death-bed recurred to his mind

ith vivid force. There was a reproach in it which he
)uld not banish or avoid. At length he sank into his
:m-chair, coughing and groaning, and averting his eyes
om Phœbe. She was accustomed to his humours, and she
ood at the table patiently, biding his time.

"You have made me forget what I was about to say," he
egan.

"I am sorry, father."

"You are not sorry; you are glad. You are always
iwarting and going against me. What makes you speak
) me of your mother in a voice of reproach? Tell me
iat. You have been egged on to it!" And he thumped
is crutch stick viciously on the floor.

"I have not been egged on to it," said Phœbe, with
)irit; "and it is entirely a fancy of yours that I spoke in
tone of reproach."

"It is no fancy; I am never wrong—never. Your
iother died when you were almost a baby in arms. You
ave no remembrance of her; it isn't possible that you can
:member her."

"I do not remember her, father," said Phœbe, with a

7—2

touch of sadness in her tone; "but Aunt Leth has a portrait of her, which I often and often look at, and I am glad
to know that I am like her. You surely can't be displeased
at that?"

"Aunt Leth! Aunt Leth! Aunt Leth!" he exclaimed,
fretfully; and then, with unreasonable vehemence, "Why
do you try to irritate me?"

"I do not try," said Phœbe, "and I do not thwart and
go against you."

"You do—in everything. You don't care to please me;
you don't take the least trouble to carry out my wishes.
Being confined, on and off, to this house for years by my
cursed rheumatism, unable, as you know, to go to my
London office, and forced to trust to a man who may be
robbing me secretly all the time he is in my service, I have
endeavoured to train you to be of some assistance to me,
and to make up my accounts here when I am too weak and
in too much pain to make them up for myself. What has
been the result? Upon looking over the papers you have
written I have seldom found one of them correct. Nothing
but errors in the casting-up and in the calculations of in-

terest—errors which would have been the ruin of me had I taken your work for granted. It wouldn't matter so much if your mistakes were in my favour, but they are not; they are always against me. The sum total is always too little instead of too much. Is this what I have a right to expect from a child I have nourished and fed?"

"I can't help it, father. I have told you over and over again that I have no head for figures."

"'No head for figures!'" he muttered. "Where should *I* be, I'd like to know, if I had no head for figures? In the workhouse, where you'll drive me to in the end. You will be satisfied then—eh?"

"I *cannot* help it, father," Phœbe repeated. "I never *could* add up so as to be depended upon; I never *could* calculate interest; I never *could* subtract or multiply. If it hadn't been for Aunt Leth, I don't believe I should ever have been able to read or write at all."

"Oh, you throw that in my teeth, because I was too poor to afford a governess for you?"

"Not at all, father. You do what you think is best, I

dare say.   I only mention it out of justice to Aunt Leth, of whom you have not a good opinion."

"How do you know that?   Have I ever troubled myself about her at all?   Did I commence this, or you?   Am I in the habit of dragging her name into our conversations for the purpose of speaking ill of her?"

"Neither of speaking ill or well, father.   That is what I complain of.   After what she has done for me you might have acted differently toward her."

"Ah, it's coming now.   She *has* egged you on!"

"She has not," said Phœbe, stamping her foot; her loyal nature was deeply wounded by those shafts aimed at one she loved so well.   "She hasn't the slightest idea that I had it in my mind to speak to you at all about her, and I *have* had it in my mind for a long time past."

"I remember now what I was going to say a minute ago. We will go upon sure ground, you, I, and your precious aunt and uncle.   We will have no delusions.   They think I am rich—eh?"

"They have never said a word about your money; they are too high-minded."

"But they *do* think I am rich. Now I will let you into a secret, and you can let them into it if you like. I am not rich; I am a pauper; and when I die you will find yourself a beggar."

"Aunt Leth will give me a home, father, when it comes to that."

"That's your affection!—taking the idea of my death so coolly. But I am not going to die yet, my girl—not yet, not yet. Why, there was a man who grew to be old, much older than I am, and who was suddenly made young and handsome and well-formed, with any amount of money at his command—"

"Oh, hush, father! These are wicked thoughts. You make me tremble."

"Why do you provoke me, then?" he cried, raising his crutch stick as though he would like to strike her. "You see how I am suffering, and you haven't a spark of feeling in you. Haven't I enough to put up with already, without being irritated by my own flesh and blood? There *was* such a man, and there's no harm in speaking of him. What was his name? This infernal rheumatism drives everything out of my head.   What was his name?"

"Faust."

"You have read about him?"

"Yes; and I went to the theatre and saw the most lovely opera about it.   I can play nearly all the music in it."

"You can play, eh?   How did you manage that?   Who gave you lessons?"

"Aunt Leth.   She has a beautiful piano."

"You never to'd me you had been to the theatre."

"I have told you often that I have been with Aunt and Uncle Leth to different theatres."

"But to this particular one, where the opera was played?"

"Yes, I told you, father.   You must have forgotten it."

"The opera!   An expensive amusement which only rich people can afford.   Your aunt took you, of course?"

"Yes."

"And she is poor, eh?—so very, very poor that it is quite wonderful how she manages!"

"She had a ticket given to her for a box that almost touched the ceiling.   She could not afford to pay for it.

Every time she has taken me to a theatre it was with a ticket given to her by Uncle Leth's relations. She *is* poor."

"And I am poorer. If you have read about Faust—if you go to the theatre and see him, why do you call me wicked for simply speaking of him? Is there really any truth in it, I wonder? There are strange things in the world. *Could* life and youth be bought? If it could—if it could—" He paused, and looked around with trembling eagerness.

Phœbe was too much frightened to speak for a little while; her father's eager looks and words terrified her. In a few minutes he recovered himself, and said, coldly,

"Finish about your aunt and uncle."

"Yes, father, I will. It isn't much I want. Next Saturday is my birthday, and Uncle Leth comes home early from his bank. He has never been to Parksides; and Aunt Leth hasn't been here for years. May I ask them to come in the evening?"

"Is that all—you are sure that is all?"

"Yes, that is all."

Miser Farebrother felt as if a great weight had been lifted

from his heart.   He had been apprehensive that Phœbe intended to ask him to lend them a sum of money.

" They wished me," said Phœbe, " to spend my birthday at their house ; but I thought I *should* like them to come here instead.   They made a party for me last year, and the year before last too ; and it is so mean to be always taking and never giving."

" I don't agree with you.   If people like to give, it shows they get a pleasure out of it, and it is folly to prevent them. But if you've set your heart upon it, Phœbe—"

" Yes, I have, father."

" Well, you can ask them ; unless," he added, with a sudden suspicion, "you have already arranged every-thing."

" Nothing is arranged.   Thank you, father."

" They will come after tea, I suppose ?"

" No," said Phœbe, blushing for shame ; " they will come before tea."

" Will they bring it with them ? "

"Oh, father ! "

" What do you mean by ' Oh, father !' ?   *I* can't afford

to give parties. *I* can't afford to go to the theatres. If people have orders given to them, they have to pay for them somehow."

"I can give them a cup of tea, surely, father?"

"I suppose you must," he grumbled. "We shall have to make up for it afterward. What are you looking at me so strangely for?"

"I should like to buy a cake for tea," said Phœbe, piteously; she was almost ready to cry, but she tried to force a smile as she added, "and I have just twopence for my fortune. Look, father: here is my purse. That won't pay for a cake, will it? Give me something for a birthday present."

"To waste in cakes," he said, with a wry face. "Where should I have been if I had been so reckless? But you'll worry me to death, I suppose, if I refuse." He unlocked a drawer, and took out a little packet, which he untied. There were ten two-shilling pieces in it, and he gave Phœbe one of them, weighing them first in his hand, and selecting the lightest and oldest. "There. Never tell anybody that I am not generous to you."

Phœbe turned the florin over in the palm of her hand, and eyed it dubiously; but she brightened up presently, and kissing her father, left the room with a cheerful face.

CHAPTER VIII

A DAY-DREAMER IN LONDON STREETS.

Now as to the Lethbridges, concerning whose characters and peculiarities it is necessary to say something more.

There was Mrs. Lethbridge, whom we already know, affectionately called Aunt Leth, not only by Phœbe, but by a great many young people who were on terms of friendship with her. And to be on such terms with such a woman was worth while, for she was not only a magnet that attracted love, she was a sun that bestowed it. There was Mr. Lethbridge, for the same reason called Uncle Leth by his young friends, and delighted in being so called. There was Fanny Lethbridge, their only daughter, between whom and Phœbe passed, under the seal of sacred secrecy, the most delicious confidences. Lastly, there was Robert Lethbridge, their only son, a young gentleman of vague and unlimited views, just entering into the serious business of life, and who, when things were perfectly smooth between him and his cousin Phœbe, was addressed as Bob, and at other times, according to the measure of dignity deemed neces-sary, as Robert or Cousin Robert. But it was generally Bob.

Mrs. Lethbridge, on her last birthday, forty-four; Mr. Lethbridge, on *his* last birthday, forty-eight; Fanny on *her* last birthday, nineteen (with many a sigh at being compelled to bid farewell to teens); Robert, on *his* last birthday, twenty-two. These comprised the family.

To hark back for a moment. It was an undoubted love match with Aunt and Uncle Leth. He a bank clerk, with limited income; she a young lady, with no income at all. That was of small account, however. Cupid—the real one, not the counterfeit—does not pause to consider. They had a boundless income in their love, and they drew large checks upon it. Expectations they had none, except that of being happy. Unlike the majority of expectations, theirs was fulfilled.

Outwardly and inwardly happy. For instance: their honey-moon. Was there ever a honey-moon like it, though it was not spent on the Continent? Never. It was their opinion, and if you dispute it you do so upon insufficient evidence. Then, their children. Parents never drew sweeter delight from their offspring than they from theirs. It is a species of delight which cannot be bought, being far more precious than silver and gold, and in the hourly and daily return for love invested it proclaims itself an incomparable speculation. Robert came first, Fanny next. This was as it should be. The boy to protect the girl, who of the two was infinitely the wiser. This is often the case with boys and girls.

The loving couple had a hard fight of it, and much to learn. They buckled to with willingness and cheerfulness, took their rubs lightly, and spread their pleasures so that they lasted a long time—not making light of them, as some do, and thus depriving themselves of the greater part of the enjoyment to be derived from them. As an example : a visit to the theatre, for which they were now able to obtain "orders." But it was not so during the first years of their married life. The contemplated visit used to be planned weeks beforehand—-discussed, laughed over, enjoyed in the anticipation, but not half so much as in the realization. As to which theatre, now, and which play? The grave conversations they had on the point! It was really worth while listening to them. Those nights were gala-nights. After the theatre, a bit of supper, perhaps—occasionally, but rarely—in a restaurant. The careful study of the bill of fare; the selection of the modest dishes; the merry words with which they banished the expensive ones and chose the cheapest—nothing could be more delightful, nothing more truly enjoyable. They went out to meet the sun, and revelled in its beams. Worth laying to heart, this!

Their income of a hundred and eighty sufficed. They could not save money—but what a mine was the future!

Of the two, the one who drew most largely upon it was Mr. Lethbridge. The extraordinary demands he made upon it, and the extraordinary readiness with which his demands were met! It will be not unpleasant to linger a little over this phase of his character, premising, for lucidity, that in all London could not be found a brighter, more agreeable day-dreamer.

Thus : Walking to the bank to save the 'bus fare, Mr.
ethbridge beguiled the way.   He had kissed his wife and
ınny, and saw them smiling at the window, and waving
eir hands to him as he passed the house.   He went on his
ıy rejoicing, and straightway began to dream.

What is this he hears ?   A meeting of the bank directors
being held.   A messenger appears before Mr. Leth-
idge's desk.

" The directors wish to see you, sir."

He prepares to obey the call, leaves his papers and books
order, pulls up his shirt collar, pulls down his cuffs,
·aightens himself generally, and presents himself in the
ard-room.   There they are, the great magnates, all before
m.   The chairman, white-haired, gold-spectacled, and
easant-voiced.   Others of the directors also white-haired,
ld-spectacled, and pleasant-voiced.   Comfortable-looking
ntlemen of the highest respectability, with country houses,
rriages and horses, first-class railway tickets, and famous
llars of wine—all plainly visible in their shirt fronts and
ld watch chains.   They gaze at him in approval.   He
ws to them.   The chairman bends his head slightly, and

smiles a welcome. The other directors follow suit. They bend their heads slightly, and smile a welcome. It is really very pleasant.

"Take a seat, Mr. Lethbridge. We wish to say a few words to you."

He sinks into a chair, and waits for the chairman to unfold himself. The chairman coughs to clear his voice.

"You have served the bank, Mr. Lethbridge, man and boy, for twenty-eight years. We have observed you for many years, and are happy to express our approval of the manner in which you have performed your duties."

What could be better than that? How delighted they will be at home when he tells them!

"Always punctual at your post, Mr. Lethbridge. Never an error in your accounts. We have had no occasion to complain of the slightest irregularity."

Positive facts, and, although not mentioned till now, carefully noted by those in authority over him. Of that there could be no doubt; and how pleasant and agreeable it was to hear it! He had always been confident that his time would come.

"As a substantial mark of our approval, Mr. Lethbridge, we offer you the desk of our second chief cashier, who is about to retire on a pension. You will take his place at the end of the present month, and your salary will be six hundred pounds per annum."

The chairman rises and shakes hands with him; the other directors rise and shake hands with him. He retires from the board room, filled with joy. Everybody in the bank congratulates him; he has not an enemy in the establishment.

Being now in the enjoyment of a salary more than three times as large as that upon which he and his wife have had to manage since their marriage, he proceeds to the disposal of it. A little extravagance is allowable; he must work down his feelings somehow. A new dress suit for himself, a new black silk for his wife. His dress suit had lasted him for Heaven knows how long, and his wife's black silk has been made over and turned till it really could not be made over and turned again. Bob shall have the gold watch he has been promised since childhood, and which father's ship —which certainly has made one of the longest passages on record—has been bringing home for the last dozen years. Fanny shall be suitably provided for. For wife and daughter, each one dozen pairs of kid gloves, four button, eight button, a hundred button if they like; new bonnets, mantles, and boots; and also for each a ten-pound note, in a new purse, to do just as they please with. Phœbe, also, must not be forgotten. She shall have new gloves, and bonnet, and mantle, and boots, and money in a new purse. He goes out with them to make the purchases, and they have the most delightfully grave consultations and discussions. And just as the shopkeeper in Regent street is pressing upon him a most extraordinary bargain in the shape of a new silk——

Yes, just at that moment Mr. Lethbridge arrives at the bank, punctual, as usual, to the minute. He is in the best of spirits. His walk from Camden Town has been as good as a play. Better; for he is convinced that his dreams will come true one of these fine days. What does it matter, a week or two sooner or later?

CHAPTER IX.

A NEW DOMESTIC DRAMA, BY UNCLE LETH.

ON the evening of the day on which Phœbe received from her father the gift of a florin, which munificent sum he deemed to be sufficient to provide for his daughter's birthday treat to her aunt and uncle Leth and her cousins, Mr. Lethbridge wended his way homeward from the bank, indulging, as he walked, in a more than usually glowing daydream. There exists in a great number of poor and struggling families a common sympathetic legend of a relation who ran away from home when very young, who has made a fabulous fortune in a distant land, and who will one day suddenly present himself to his astonished kinsfolk, and fill their hearts with joy by pouring untold gold into their laps. This good genius is always a gray-headed old man, with bright eyes and a soul of good-nature, and is, of course, invariably a bachelor—a delightful fiction which insures comfortable portions to the marriageable girls. " The Indies" used to be the favourite locality in which the runaway uncle or cousin made and saved his fortune, but of late years Australia and America have been pressed into service. Such a legend had existed in Mr. Lethbridge's family when he was a youngster ; and as he now walked toward Camden Town, who should turn up—in his dreams—but a fabulously wealthy old gentleman, who had come home for the express purpose of presenting Mr. Lethbridge with no less a sum than twenty thousand pounds ? Here was a foundation for the day-dreamer to work upon ! but it was not all. There was a most important connection nearer to his heart, and altogether of a more tangible character. Among the friends of the family was a certain Fred Cornwall, a young barrister waiting for briefs, regarding whom Mrs. Lethbridge had more than once confidentially unbosomed herself to her spouse to the effect that she was certain "he came after Fanny." Up to the present moment, supposing that Fred Cornwall had really any serious intentions, this was as far as he had got ; but it was far enough for Mr. Lethbridge. The slenderest foundations were sufficiently strong for his castles. Now, on this evening, Fred Cornwall was abroad on a little summer trip, and before Mr. Lethbridge had started for his bank in the morning his wife had whispered to him that Fanny had received a letter from Fred. What more was wanting for fancy with open eyes in London streets?

He has left the bank. They gave him a dinner and a testimonial on parchment, and another in gold, which is now ticking in the left-hand pocket of his waistcoat. It was the pleasantest affair. Such things were said of him! And the choicest flowers from the banquet table were sent by hand to his wife and daughter. Simply to think of it made the tears come into his eyes.

He has bought the lease of the dear old house in Camden Town. He has no ambition to live in a better, despite the fact that he is master of twenty thousand pounds. Well, not quite so much, perhaps, because there was the lease to pay for, and the smartening up of the house, and some new furniture to buy for the best rooms. But quite enough, quite enough.

There is still something to do before the new arrangements are completed, and for this purpose he and his wife and Fanny are jogging along happily through fashionable thoroughfares, where the tradesmen have provided in their windows a veritable Aladdin's cave for their entertainment, and wherein the ladies of his family, intent upon killing two birds with one stone, have decided to indulge in a " little shopping"—of all female occupations the most attractive and fascinating.

In Regent Street whom should they meet but Fred Cornwall? Here he is, face to face with them. Mr. Lethbridge greets him cordially.

"Hallo, Fred! Who would have thought of seeing you? Why, where have you been these last three weeks? On the Continent? Of course, of course—I remember your telling us you were going. Enjoyed yourself, I hope? Yes! Very glad, very glad. · How brown you look! When did you return? A few hours ago only—ah! Come round and see us this evening. You intended to! That's right. You'll see an improvement—we've been buying some new furniture and doing up the house. Do you know anything of roses, Fred? I want to put a few dozen standards in the garden ; I've got some apple and pear trees in already.   Our

own fruit next year, Fred.   Fact is, I've had a windfall.

Ever heard me tell of a relation of mine who ran away from

home when he was a boy, and who made a great fortune

abroad ?   Well, to our astonishment, he turned up a little

while ago, and behaved most handsomely to us ; so handsomely, indeed, that I've resigned at the bank.   No occasion to work any more, my boy ; can take it easy.   Pleased

to hear it ?   Of course you are.   It makes no difference in

us, Fred.   We're just the same as we always were—just the

same—just the same.   Now how about the briefs, Fred ?

Are they rolling in ?   No !   But of course you must wait,

as I have waited.   Don't be discouraged, my lad !   Hope

—hope—hope ;   that's   the   best   tonic   for   youngsters.

Perhaps I may put something in your way.   Anything particular to do this morning?   We are making a few purchases, and, now I think of it, I have heard Fanny say,

repeatedly, that your taste in ladies' dress is perfect.   What

are you blushing for, Fanny?   Give Fred your arm.   I have

no doubt he will be happy to accompany us."

Mr. Lethbridge's day-dream was here snapped in the

middle. He was recalled to earth by a clap on his shoulder and the sound of a mellow voice.

" The very man I was coming to see! How are you, Leth, old man ? "

The mellowness of the speaker's voice was matched by the mellowness of his personal appearance. Good spirits and good-nature oozed out of him. His clean-shaven face was round and rubicund; his eyes had a cheery light in them; a jolly smile hovered about his mouth. He was a large man; his hands, his nose, his head, were massive—it is the only word that will describe them. But nothing in him was out of proportion, and the geniality and jollity of the man were in keeping with his physical gifts. As there is no occasion for mystery, he may at once be introduced : " Mr. Kislingbury—the reader."

A famous man, Mr. Kislingbury, as you know. Has he not afforded you opportunities innumerable, of which, as a sensible man, you have taken full advantage—for it is not to be doubted that you are an enthusiastic play-goer—for hearty laughter? Has he not made your sides ache this many a time and oft, and have you not gone home the

better for it ?   Is there not something so contagious in the
merry notes of his rich voice that your mouth wreathes
with smiles the moment it reaches your ears?   Yes, everybody knows Kiss—though his name be Kislingbury, he is
never spoken of but as Kiss by his friends and the public—
and everybody has a kindly feeling toward him.   With
reason.   His humour is unctuous, but never coarse ; he bub-
bles over with fun, but never descends to buffoonery ; great
in old comedies, to the manner born, and, perhaps because
of that, a little out of date.   But Kiss, although fortune has
not been over-lavish toward him, is contented with his lot.
And he has, perhaps, a rarer virtue than all—he respects
his author, and when he plays a new part and makes a hit in
it, does not take all the credit to himself.   This is the man
who clapped Mr. Lethbridge on the shoulder in the midst
of that gentleman's glowing day-dream, and cried : " The
very man I was coming to see !   How are you, Leth, old
man ? "

"Very well, I thank you," said Mr. Lethbridge, a little
slowly, not immediately recognizing his friend ; he was not
in the habit of taking a harlequin leap out of his musings ;

it generally occupied him a few moments to get back to earth. "Very well, very well. Why, it's Kiss! Glad to see you, Kiss, glad to see you!"

"Day-dreaming, Leth?" inquired Kiss, merrily and kindly.

Mr. Lethbridge's flights in this direction were well-known to his friends.

"Yes, Kiss, yes. Amusing myself as usual. Upon my word, I hardly know a better way of passing the time. Almost as good as a theatre."

Kiss and Mr. Lethbridge were related—second or third cousins, or something of that sort; one of those genealogical connections with mixed marriages which make the head ache—and it was from Kiss that Mr. Lethbridge obtained orders for the play. Kiss had other and nearer relations, some of whom were in the habit of visiting Mr. Lethbridge's house, where, it need scarcely be said, they were more than welcome, the younger members of Aunt Leth's family, and all her other young friends, looking up to these luminaries with a kind of awe.

"Better than a theatre, I dare say," said Kiss, heartily;

"at all events, a great deal cheaper. So easy to get up your pieces, so easy to write 'em, so easy to get them played. No jealousies and heart-burnings ; all plain sailing. And no rehearsals, my boy ; no rehearsals "—at which contemplation Kiss joyously rubbed his hands. " Everybody pleased and satisfied with his part. Lessee, stage-manager, every soul in the place, down to the check-taker at the gallery—I should rather say up, shouldn't I ?—in a state of calm beatitude. Why ? Because success is assured beforehand. No expense for dresses, none for scenery. Such a first-night audience ! No blackguards paying their shillings in the hope of a chance of hooting and hissing. There are such now-a-days, I regret to say. Then the critics ! Not at all a bad lot, Leth, let me tell you, though they have given many a poor devil the heartache. I often pity them for the sorry stuff they have to listen to and write about. Not a bed of roses, theirs ! And I'd sooner be Kiss, first low comedy, than dramatic critic of the best paper going. As you play your pieces, Leth, do you ever think of the fine notices written about 'em in the next morning's papers ? "

"I seldom get as far as that," replied Mr. Lethbridge, smiling.

"Ah!" said Kiss, "that's because you have no vanity."

"I have a great deal," said Mr. Lethbridge, shaking his head.

"You're no judge of yourself: none of us are of ourselves. But let your mind run on it a bit; it will make your nerves tingle with delight. Not for yourself, perhaps; for others— for Aunt Leth, now; and pretty Fanny; and Bob, the rascal!"

"Yes, for them, for them!" said Mr. Lethbridge, eagerly. "I will, Kiss; I will!—that is, if it comes to me to do it. For, do you know, what you call 'my pieces' are really very curious things, not only in themselves, but in the way they happen. Quite unexpectedly, Kiss—quite unexpectedly. Now what do the critics say about the piece—just by way of example—I've been playing in my walk home from the bank? But its rather foolish of me to ask you such a question, as you are in complete ignorance of the kind of piece it is."

" Wrong, Leth, wrong. I know a great deal about it ; more than you are aware of."

" Really ? "

" Really, and in very truth, my liege lord."

" Now this is interesting. It is quite a pleasure, meeting you in this way. Go on about my piece."

"First and foremost," said Kiss, " to settle the style of it. I pronounce that it is not a tragedy."

" Right ; it is not."

" It is not a farce."

" Nothing like it—that is, broadly speaking."

" I am speaking broadly. It is not a blood-thirsty melo-drama, with a murder in it, and a wedding ; or, if not that, a pair of lovers, just about to be tied together ; or, if not that, a husband and wife torn from each other's arms. It amounts to the same thing, because the main point is that the man is falsely accused of the murder."

" Of course he is, said Mr. Lethbridge, " or where should we be ? "

" Exactly," said Kiss, with a humorous imitation of Mr. Lethbridge's manner. " If that was not the case, where should we be? Worth considering. Perhaps worse off; perhaps better. I will not take it upon myself to judge. We are talking now of the regulation pattern—good old style, Leth, *but* old. Would stand a bad chance if it were not for the magnificent scenery and the wonderful dresses, mechanical changes, houses turned inside out, exteriors turned outside in, gas lowered to vanishing point to assist the delusion—splendid opportunity that for the lover and his lass, in the pit ! Wish I was young again, and before the foot-lights, instead of behind them, so that I might take my imaginary little girl (whom I adore, from the crown of her pretty head to the tips of her little shoes) to the pit when such a melodrama, with the lights turned down, is being played. When I say 'regulation pattern,' Leth, don't mistake me; I am not speaking against it. As for originality— well, perhaps the least said about it the better. We were rehearsing a new melodrama the other day, and the subject cropped up on the stage. The scene-painter was there, and he took part in the discussion, though he spoke never a word."

"How could he do that without speaking?"

" Well, he winked."

" I don't see much in that," observed Mr. Lethbridge, somewhat mystified.

" Of course you don't, the reason being "—and good humour beamed in every feature of Kiss's merry face— "that you are not, like myself, a cynic."

" Come, that's good," protested Mr. Lethbridge : " you a cynic ! "

" I would not have my enemies say so," said Kiss ; "and don't you betray me at home. So it is settled that your piece is not a tragedy, nor a broad farce, nor a melodrama with a murder in it. Nor is it a comedy of character, bristling with smart sayings—everybody saying clever, ill-natured things about everybody else. No, Leth ; *your* piece is a simple domestic drama, lighted up by the sweetest stars of life—the stars of pure love and a happy home."

" You have," said Mr. Lethbridge, stirred by the feeling which his friend threw into the words, " a remarkable felicity of expression. You are almost — a poet."

"A bread-and-butter poet, then. Yes; a simple drama of domestic life, upon which the stars of love and home are shining. That's what the critics say the next morning: ' It is refreshing to come across a play so sweet, so natural, so human. Here are no high flights of the imagination ; no violent twisting of ordinary events to serve a startling purpose ; no dragging in of abnormal, precocious children, to show how clever they are ; nothing, in short, out of drawing or out of proportion. The play is an idyl, in which all that is wholesome in every-day life is brought into prominence to gladden the heart and refresh the senses. It leaves a sweet taste in the mouth, and when the curtain fell upon the delightful story, the author was called again and again, and applauded with a heartiness which must have sent him home rejoicing to the bosom of his family. We trust that the success he won and deserved will encourage him to further efforts in this direction, and that on many future occasions he will charm and beguile us as he did last night. His feet are firmly planted on the ladder of fame, and he has only to go on as he has begun, to make his name a household word.' "

"Upon my word," said Mr. Lethbridge, "you almost take away my breath."

"But am I a true diviner?" asked Kiss.

"About the critics?"

"About the piece—*your* piece?"

"You are a wizard. I think if I *were* a dramatic author I should try to write precisely the kind of play you have described. You see, there is little else in my mind. But I am afraid you are wrong about the critics."

"Not at all," persisted Kiss. "Critics are human, like other people; and search the whole world through, you will find no song more popular than 'Home, sweet Home.'"

CHAPTER X.

WHILE this conversation was proceeding there stood at a little distance from the speakers a man who had been walking arm in arm with the actor when the friends met, and who fell apart from Kiss when he clapped Mr. Lethbridge upon the shoulder. He was an anxious-eyed man, nervous, fidgety, with a certain tremulousness of limb and feature, denoting a troubled nature. His age was some thirty-five or thereabouts ; his clothes were respectable and shabby; and although he took no part in the conversation, and did not obtrude himself, he did not remove his eyes from Kiss and Mr. Lethbridge. Kiss, turning, beckoned to him, and he joined the friends.

"You heard what we've been talking about," said the actor. " What do you think of it ? "

"I wish," said the man, "that I could write such a piece."

"Ah," said Kiss, "it is easy to preach as we've been preaching, but to do the thing is a different pair of shoes. It comes by nature, or it comes not at all."

"But," said the man, "I don't believe it would be a success."

"Wait a moment," said Kiss; "I am forgetting my manners. Mr. Linton—Mr. Lethbridge."

The two shook hands.

"Mr. Linton," said Kiss to Mr. Lethbridge, in explana· tion, "*is* a dramatic author, and has written plays."

Mr. Linton sighed, and fidgeted with his fingers.

"Has he?" exclaimed Mr. Lethbridge.   "And they have been played, of course ?"

Mr. Linton sighed again, and inclined his head.

"I am really delighted," said Mr. Lethbridge.   "I have never in my life spoken to a dramatic author, and have never shaken hands with one.   Will you allow me ?"

They shook hands again, Mr. Lethbridge effusively, Mr. Linton with mingled bashfulness, pride, and awkwardness.

· "Successful pieces, I am sure," observed Mr. Leth· bridge

" More or less so," said Kiss. " We must take our rubs, my dear Leth."

" Of course, of course. We've got to take them."

" That's what I'm always telling Linton. We've got to take 'em. Why, you, now," pointing his finger at Mr. Lethbridge, " you're not a public man, and you have your rubs."

" I am not free from them," said Mr. Lethbridge, in a cheerful voice.

" There, now, Linton," said Kiss, with the manner of one who desired to point a moral, " our friend Lethbridge here is not a public man, and *he* has rubs. So you don't think his piece would be a success ? Why, Sempronius ? "

" An author must follow the fashion," replied Mr. Linton, " if he wants to live."

" He wants that, naturally." And here Kiss took Mr. Lethbridge aside, with, " Excuse me, Linton, a moment," and whispered, confidentially, " A little dashed. Had a knock-down blow. Last piece a failure. Produced a fort-night ago. Ran a week. I was in it, but could not save it. Consequence, out of an engagement ; not serious to me, but to him—very. A man of genius ; but not yet hit 'em quite. Will soon, or I'm the worst of actors. Which I am not—nor the best ; but 'twill serve. Meanwhile, waiting for the spondulix to pour in, has wife and family to support. A modern Triplet. Has play which will take the town by storm. The play that failed was of a domestic turn. Very pretty ; but lacked incident. Too much dialogue, too little action. He feels it—badly. Here," touching his heart, "and here," touching his stomach. They returned to Mr. Linton. " Proceed, Linton."

"The public," said Mr. Linton, "require red fire. Give it them. They want murders. Supply them. They want the penny-dreadful on the stage. Fling it at their heads. Ah ! I've not been as wise as some I know."

" In point of ability," whispered Kiss again to Mr. Lethbridge, "he could wipe out the authors he refers to. Excuse him ; he is not a bit malicious or envious ; but he has been stung, and he's writhing. If you heard me read the play that failed, you would require a dozen pocket-handkerchiefs. He slaved at it for eight months ; and dreamt of success with empty platters on his table. I wonder if people know anything of this, or ever give it a thought? But it won't do to encourage him. It does him good to lash out; but we must not agree with him when he's wrong. In his new play there's a part I should like to take. He wrote it with me in his eye. All will come right; till the time arrives, he must grin and bear it. ' Suffering is the badge of all his tribe.' But there are big plums in the pudding, old fellow, and his day to pick 'em will come." Then he said aloud to the moody author: " Don't talk stuff and nonsense. You don't copy, as a rule; you're original, and I make my bow to you; but in what you said you *are* copying the platitudinarians. What the public want are good plays, such as you can write, and good actors, who are not so scarce as croakers would have us believe. Cheer up, Linton! Where would be the glory of success if we could have it by whistling for it? Why, here we are at your very door, Leth! Now I call that singular."

" Why? " asked Mr. Lethbridge.

" Because we were coming to see you, to ask a favour."

" Anything I can do," said Mr. Lethbridge, knocking at the door, "you may depend upon."

" I told you so, Linton," said Kiss.

The dramatic author brightened up for a moment, but fell again immediately into a state of despondency.

" You're just in time for tea," said Mr. Lethbridge, kissing his wife, who opened the door for them. "Come in, come in. I've brought you some visitors, mother.".

" How do you do, Mr. Kiss?" said Mrs. Lethbridge, shaking hands with the always welcome actor.

" Mother," said Mr. Lethbridge, " this is Mr. Linton, the celebrated author."

" I am glad to see you, sir," said Mrs. Lethbridge, inwardly disturbed by the thought that she had not got out her best tea service. " Mr. Kiss, will you take Mr. Linton into the drawing-room? You are at home, you know. Fanny and Bob will be in presently. Phœbe is here, father."

In point of fact, Phœbe, Fanny, and Bob, excited by the sound of the arrival of visitors, were on the first-floor landing, peeping over the balustrade to see who they were.

" It's Mr. Kiss," whispered Fanny.

" And a strange gentleman," whispered Bob.

"Uncle Leth said," whispered Phœbe, "'the celebrated author.' I wonder if he's joking?"

"They are going to stop to tea," whispered Fanny, "and mother has sent them into the drawing-room while she gets out the best tea-things. We must go and help her."

Aunt Leth, from the passage below, coughed aloud, having detected the presence of the young people, and there was an instant scuttling away above, and a sound of smothered laughter. To Aunt Leth's relief, this was not noticed by her visitors, who made their way into the drawing-room. It was called so more from habit than because it was a room set apart for holiday and grand occasions; there was no such room in the house of the Lethbridges, which was a home in the truest sense of the word.

Aunt Leth was deeply impressed by the circumstance of having a celebrated author in her house, and when the drawing-room door was closed, she asked her husband in the passage—speaking in a very low tone—what he had written.

"Why, don't you know, mother?" said Mr. Lethbridge; but the superior air he assumed—as though he was intimately acquainted with everything Mr. Linton had written, and was rather surprised at his wife's question—was spoilt by a shamefacedness which he was not clever enough to conceal.

"No, father," said Mrs. Lethbridge; adding, triumphantly, "and I don't believe you do, either."

"Well, to tell you the truth," said Mr. Lethbridge, with a little laugh, "I don't. But he *is* very celebrated. Mr. Kiss says so. He writes plays, and his last one was not a success. It has troubled him greatly, poor fellow. Give us a good tea, mother."

Mrs. Lethbridge nodded, and sent him in to his visitors, and went herself down to the kitchen to attend to her domestic arrangements, where she was presently joined by her children and Phœbe.

"We don't want you, Bob," said Mrs. Lethbridge to her son; "go and join the gentlemen."

"I'd sooner stop here, mother," said Robert.

"Go away, there's a good boy," said the mother; "you will only put things back."

Robert, however, showed no inclination to leave the

kitchen, but hovered about Phœbe like a butterfly about a flower.

"*Do* you hear what mother says?" demanded Fanny, imperiously; she was given to lord it occasionally over her brother. "Go at once, and listen to the gentlemen, and have your mind improved."

"Now you're chaffing me," said Robert, "and you know that always puts my back up."

Mrs. Lethbridge looked around with affectionate distraction in her aspect.

"Go, Robert," said Phœbe.

"Not if you call me 'Robert,'" said he.

"Well, Bob."

"All right, I'll vanish. Fanny, there's a smut on your nose."

Which caused Fanny to rub that feature smartly with her handkerchief, and then to ask Phœbe in a tone of concern, "Is it off?" This sent Robert from the kitchen laughing, while Fanny called out to him that she would pay him for it. She laughed too, when he was gone, and declared that he was getting a greater tease every day. Presently all was bustle ; the best cups and saucers were taken from the cupboard, and Phœbe, with her sleeves tucked up, was dusting them ; Fanny was cutting the bread and buttering it ; Aunt Leth was busy with eggs and rashers of bacon, and the frying-pan was on the fire ; while, attending to the frying-pan and the kettle and the teapot, and working away generally with a will, was the most important person in the kitchen—the goddess, indeed, of that region—whose name, with a strange remissness, has not yet been mentioned : 'Melia Jane !

In these days of fine-lady-servants, the mere mention of so inestimable a treasure is an agreeable thing ; for if ever there was a devoted, untiring, unselfish, capable, cheerful slave of the broom and the pan, that being was 'Melia Jane. Up early in the morning, without ever being called ; up late at night, without a murmur ; no Sundays out, as a law, the violation of which was a graver matter than the separation of church and state ; cooking, scrubbing, washing, with a light heart, and as happy as the day is long. Could I write an epic, I would set about it, and call it " 'Melia Jane."

Not a beauty ; somewhat the reverse, indeed. But

"Lor!" as she used to say, scratching her elbow, "beauty's only skin-deep." Nevertheless, she worshipped it in the persons of Fanny and Phœbe, to whom she was devotedly attached. Of the two, she leaned, perhaps, more closely and affectionately to Phœbe, for whom she entertained the profoundest admiration, "Wenus," she declared, "couldn't 'old a candle to 'er." And had she been asked, in the way of disputation, under what circumstances and to what intelligible purpose that goddess could be expected to hold a candle to Phœbe, she would doubtless have been prepared with a reply which would have confounded the interrogator.

She had a history, which can be briefly recorded.

Like all careful housewives with limited incomes, Mrs. Lethbridge had her washing "done" at home, and 'Melia Jane's mother, in times gone by, was Aunt Leth's washerwoman. She died when 'Melia Jane was ten years old, and the child, being friendless and penniless, was admitted into Mrs. Lethbridge's kitchen as a kind of juvenile help. She proved to be so clever and willing, and so "teachable," as Mrs. Lethbridge said, that when the old servant left to get married, 'Melia Jane took her place, and trom that day did the entire work of the house. For the present, this brief record is sufficient. More of 'Melia Jane anon.

Robert burst into the kitchen in a state of great excitement.

" Mother, you didn't tell me Mr. Linton was a dramatic author. Just think, Phœbe; he writes plays! Isn't it grand?"

The girls opened their eyes very wide. There was indeed a luminary in the house, a star of the first magnitude. A dramatic author! It was enough to make them tremble.

" But why have you left them, Bob?" asked Mrs. Lethbridge.

" I was told to go," replied Robert. "They did not want me. They're talking business."

" Business!" exclaimed Mrs. Lethbridge. " What business can they have with father?"

" Perhaps," suggested Robert, " he is going to take a theatre, and Mr. Linton is going to write the plays, and Mr. Kiss is going to act in them."

" What nonsense you talk!" said Mrs. Lethbridge.

"Mother," said Robert, solemnly, "my mind's made up."

"A very small parcel," remarked Fanny, thus paying him off for the smut on her nose.

"I'm serious," said Robert; "I'm fixed—yes, fixed as the polar star. That sounds well. I shall go on the stage."

"And off again, very quick," said Fanny.

"What! turn actor, Bob?" exclaimed Mrs. Lethbridge.

"Yes," said Robert, folding his arms; "a second Irving."

"Avaunt, and quit my sight!" cried Phœbe, seizing the rolling-pin and striking an attitude.

They all fell to laughing, and 'Melia Jane stared at the young people, with her eyes almost starting out of their sockets.

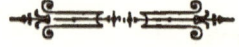

CHAPTER XI.

MEANWHILE the gentlemen upstairs were discussing a serious subject.

"I told you about our friend's play," said Kiss to Mr Lethbridge—"his undeservedly unsuccessful play, produced a fortnight since at the Star Theatre. There are lines in it which would make the fortune of a poet, but these are not poetical days—on the stage. At a certain theatre, where an eminent brother of the craft, to whom I take off my hat"—he had no hat to take off, but he went through the necessary action—"has the ear of the public, and a following which is simply amazing to contemplate—at that theatre, I grant you, the poetical drama can be produced with great results; and also at one other temple of the drama, where a lady, admired and loved by all, reigns as queen; but produced elsewhere, it is risky, very. It requires, for success, a perfect and harmonious combination of rare forces, and such a following as I have spoken of, and these are only to be found in those two theatres. Do you take?"

"Do I understand you?" said Mr. Lethbridge, deeply interested. "Yes."

"With *such* actors," continued Kiss, "with *such* an organization, with *such* resources, with *such* lavish, but not unwise, expenditure, with *such* a following, not only the poetical drama, but any kind of drama, may be staged with assured result. Had Linton's play been produced *there*, you would see him now all smiles instead of down in the dumps. I don't say to him 'What is the use?' A man has his feelings, and a dramatic author has a double share, which makes it bad for him when the reverse happens. Linton's play was not produced at one of the theatres I have indicated—more's the pity. But a time may come. Do you hear me, Linton?"

"I am deeply grateful to you," said Mr. Linton. "You are the best fellow in the world."

"That is sentiment, mere sentiment," said Kiss, coughing down the compliment. "We are now talking business, and I am, so to speak, showing our mutual friend the ropes, and letting him behind the scenes. Not quite the fairy-land most people imagine. I was engaged for the run of Linton's play, and as it ran off instead of on, I am now out of an engagement. Do I blame him? Not a bit of it. He would have as much reason to blame me. You see, Leth, there are certain rules and certains fashions in our line which it is as dangerous to violate as in most lines of business. For instance, would you take a shop on the wrong side of the road?"

"No," replied Mr. Lethbridge, rather vaguely.

"There are business sides and unbusiness sides. Here, a shop is worth five hundred pounds a year; across the road it isn't worth fifty. So with theatres. Here, comedy; here, comic opera; here, melodrama; here, spectacle; here, Shakespeare and the classic; and so on, and so on. Risk the unsuitable and you come to grief. That's what we did; for I'm bound to confess that Linton was largely influenced by my advice in the matter. I had so firm a belief in the play that I thought it would score anywhere. It *did* score

10—2

at the Star, but it scored the wrong way, because it was played at the wrong theatre. A knock-down blow! What then? Why, rise, and at it again!—yes, though you get a dozen knock-down blows. Nil desperandum: that's my motto. Life's a fight. Are you waiting for a cue, Linton?"

"You are quite right in your observations," said the poor author, with a sad smile; "but it is easier for you to rise after a knock-down blow than it is with me. You are a favourite with the public; they welcome you the moment you make your appearance. The last time I appeared before them they howled at me. And it meant so much! It was not only a case of disappointed ambition and wounded vanity, but there was, at home——I beg your pardon; I scarcely know what I was about to say."

Mr. Lethbridge thought of the empty platters which Kiss had spoken of, and he gazed commiseratingly at Mr. Linton.

"Now, wouldn't you suppose," said Kiss, addressing himself to Mr. Lethbridge, "that Linton was so overwhelmed at his failure that he had no heart to try again? I am happy to say that is not the case. He has already got another play ready, a better one than the last, a play that is bound to hit 'em ? "

" I am delighted to hear it," said Mr. Lethbridge, with a bright smile. " I must come the first night ; we'll all come —mother and Fanny and Phœbe and Bob. I dare say we shall be able to find room in the pit."

" Plenty," observed Mr. Linton, moodily.

" And bring good thick sticks with you," said Kiss, " to help the applause."

" When is it to be played," asked Mr. Lethbridge, laughing at the suggestion of the big sticks, " and where ? "

" Ah," said Kiss, " that's the rub. It is a question not yet decided."

" There are so many managers after it, I suppose ? " said Mr. Lethbridge, innocently. " Look at it from a business point of view ; accept the best offer at the best theatre."

Kiss leant back in his chair, and laughed long and loud. He had a particularly merry laugh, and the sound was heard in the kitchen.

(" That's Mr. Kiss laughing," said Fanny. " The author has said something funny."

"I hope uncle will remember it," added Phœbe, "and tell us what it is. How wonderfully an author must talk, and what wonderful minds they must have ! How ever do they think of things ? ")

"The fact is, Leth," said Kiss, presently, "we have not such a choice of managers and theatres as you imagine."

"Why, surely," said Mr. Lethbridge, "they are only too ready to jump at a good play when it is offered them !"

"If I were asked," said Kiss, "who were the worst possible judges of a manuscript play, I should answer, theatrical managers. As regards Linton's last effort, which he has at the present moment in his coat pocket"—(Mr. Lethbridge knew from this remark what the great bulge was at Mr. Linton's breast, concerning which he had been rather puzzling himself; every now and then the dramatic author put his hand up to the pocket which contained his manuscript, to make sure that the precious documents were safe)—"as regards that," continued Kiss, "there is a certain obtuseness on the part of managers which has to be over-come before the new play sees the light. They have read

it, and have shaken their heads at it. Now I pit my judgment against theirs."

" So will I," said Mr. Lethbridge.

"And I say there's money and fame in Linton's last.
By-the-way, Linton, that's not at all a bad title for something—'Linton's Last.' Think of it."

" At all events," observed the despondent author, with a
lame attempt at a joke, "there would be an end of me
after that."

" Not at all, my boy ; couldn't spare you. As I said,
Leth, the managers, all but one, shake their heads at Linton's
play, and, like asses, refuse it."

" All but one," said Mr. Lethbridge. " He's a fortunate
man, whoever he is."

" He is not *quite* blind. Now, Leth, that is the real
reason of our visit to you."

" Indeed ! " said Mr. Lethbridge, in great amazement.
" I have no influence, I assure you. I wish I had; I
should be only too ready and willing to use it."

"This one manager," pursued Kiss, " who proves himself to possess some glimmering of common-sense, is,

curiously enough, the manager of the Star Theatre, where Linton's last piece was produced."

"And he wishes to produce the new one," said Mr. Leth-bridge. "That is very good of him."

"Oh, he knows what he is about, and he is awake to the fact that there is a certain fortune in the play. But, for all that, he is a downy bird—a very downy bird. He argues. Says he, 'Your last piece, Linton, was almost a crusher to me.' At which Linton's heart sinks into his shoes, and he groans, instead of meeting it lightly as he ought to do. But that is a matter of temperament. 'I had to close my theatre,' says the manager of the Star, 'not having another piece ready, and here I am paying rent for shut doors. It has cost me so much,' mentioning a sum, which my experience tells me is the actual, multiplied by four. But that's neither here nor there. The manager of the Star goes on : 'To put the new piece on will cost so much,' again mentioning a sum multiplied by four. 'What do you propose to contribute toward it if I make the venture?' 'I give you my brains,' says Linton; 'that is all I possess.' 'In that case,' says the manager, 'I am afraid it is not to be thought of. I can't afford to stand the entire risk.' I, being present at the interview, step in here. I don't intend to apologize to Linton when I tell you, Leth, that he is not fit to manage his own business. ' You *did* produce a play of Linton's,' I say to the manager —it was called *Boots and Shoes*, Leth; no doubt you remember it—'out of which you made a pot of money.' ' A small pot,' says the manager of the Star; 'a very small pot.' 'And,' says I, 'which you bought right out for the miserable sum of fifty pounds.' 'Well,' says the manager, 'that was the bargain, made with our eyes open. When I offered fifty pounds for *Boots and Shoes* I did it for the purpose of doing Linton a good turn. He was hard up at the time, and I risked the fifty on the off chance. If I make by one piece I lose by another.' 'Let us come to the point,' says I, 'about the new piece. You want something contributed toward the expense of getting it up. How much? Don't open your mouth too wide.' 'Two hundred pounds,' says he; 'not a penny less.' To tell you the truth, Leth, I thought he was going to ask for more. It isn't a very large sum, is it?"

"Not to some people," replied Mr. Lethbridge, with a cheerful smile.

"Pleased to hear you say so. There's more to tell. It is not putting down the two hundred pounds and saying good-bye to it; it will come back in less than no time. The first profits of the piece will be devoted to repaying the amount, so that there is really very little risk, if any. Having stated his conditions the manager of the Star retires, and we retire also, to consider ways and means. Now I needn't tell you, Leth, that we can just as easily lay our hands upon two hundred pounds as we can bring the man in the moon down from the skies. The question then is—how to raise it? A serious question. We consider long, and at length a bright idea flashes upon me. I have, in an indirect way, made the acquaintance of a man who discounts bills. The acquaintance is slight—very slight; but faint heart, you know, and I go to him. I will mention his name to you; but it must be done in confidence—between ourselves."

"Yes," said Mr. Lethbridge.

"His name is Pamflett—Jeremiah Pamflett."

"I know the name of Pamflett," said Mr. Lethbridge. " The father of my niece. Phœbe, who is just now on a visit to us—"

" The dearest, sweetest girl!" said Kiss, in explanation to Mr. Linton.

" Has a housekeeper of that name. Can Mr. Jeremiah Pamflett be a connexion of hers?"

"It is not unlikely," said Kiss; "to speak the truth, it is quite likely. But that is not material, is it?"

"No," said Mr. Lethbridge, with a slight pause for consideration; "I don't think it is. I believe he manages some kind of business for Phœbe's father."

" For Miser Farebrother? Yes, that is so; but he does business also on his own account. As I was saying, I go to Mr. Pamflett, and I lay the case before him; but he says he doesn't see his way to doing a bill for me and Linton without other names upon it. I run over the names of a few friends who would be willing to sign it, but Mr. Pamflett still demurs. It was then that the bright idea flashes upon me; I think of you. To come to you and ask you to lend us two hundred pounds was, of course, out of the question."

"I regret to say it would be," said Mr. Lethbridge. "Nothing would give me greater pleasure if it were in my power."

"I know, and therefore we have not come here with any such idea; but your name occurring to me while I was talking to Mr. Pamflett, I naturally mention it. He meets me instantly. He knows all about you and your family."

"He has never been here," interposed Mr. Lethbridge.

"He spoke most kindly of you, and said he had the greatest respect for you—"

"To my knowledge," again interposed Mr. Lethbridge, "I have never seen his face. I shouldn't know him from Adam if he stood before me now."

"Perhaps he knows of you through your niece. However it is, you would not have been displeased had you heard him speak of you. The upshot of the affair is that he makes a proposition by which we shall get the two hundred pounds required to produce Linton's new play. The proposition is—and bear in mind that Mr. Pamflett made it out of pure kindness, and out of the respect in which he holds you—that Linton should draw a bill at six months' date for three hundred pounds, and that you should accept it. Linton, of course, as drawer, will endorse it, and so will I. If I hand this bill to Mr. Pamflett to-morrow he will give Linton his cheque for two hundred pounds, and our friend's fortune is made. The resources of civilization, my dear Leth, are wonderful. That a mere scratch of the pen can make a name famous, can make a worthy fellow happy, can bring joy to the hearts of a good woman and her children—you will love Mrs. Linton when you know her—can snatch a man from the depths of despair—now, is it not wonderful to think of? They will bless you, they will remember you in their prayers—but I will say no more. It remains with you."

In this speech the actor's art, unconsciously exercised, made itself felt, and it penetrated the very soul of good Uncle Leth.

"It does not enter my mind," said Mr. Lethbridge to Kiss, "that you would deceive me—"

"I would cut my right hand off first."

" And therefore you will forgive me when I ask you if there is really no risk ? "

" I give you my word and honour, Leth," said Kiss, very seriously, " as a man, and, what is more, as a judge of plays, that there is not the slightest risk.   Is my opinion, as an actor and an honourable man, of any value ? "

" Of the highest value ! "

" There is not an atom of risk.   Linton has his play in his pocket : he shall read it to you—or, rather, *I* will read it to you—before we leave you to-night.   Linton is an execrable reader of his own works.   He is so nervous and fidgety and *un*dramatic that he misses every point.   If ever I feel inclined to punch his head it is when he is reading his manuscript to the company in the greenroom.   Many a good play has been rejected because of this incapacity ; many a bad play has been accepted because of the fervour and the magnetism of the author, who, carried away him- self (frequently by inordinate vanity), has carried away a theatrical manager, and actors too sometimes, and warped their judgment.   *I* will read Linton's play fairly, so that you will be able to form a proper estimate of it.   Just consider, Leth : the bill is not due for six months.   In three or four weeks at the furthest Linton's piece will be produced. The manager of the Star Theatre would like to rush it on sooner, but I shall insist upon a proper number of rehearsals. I shall stage-manage it myself, and that should be a guarantee.   Two weeks after the production of the piece I shall have the pleasure—I beg Linton's pardon : *he* will have the pleasure—of handing you the sum of three hundred pounds in a new suit of clothes.   Not the money thus clothed, but the happy author.   That will be four months before the money is to be paid to Mr. Jeremiah Pamflett.   You can keep it and use it for those four months if you wish."

"I shall pay it at once," said Mr. Lethbridge, "and get back the bill."

"Then you will do it ? "

"I will do it," said Mr. Lethbridge : "and I wish Mr. Linton every success."

"Linton, old chap," exclaimed Kiss, "your fortune's made ! "

Mr. Linton raised his eyes.   The tears were brimming over in them, and running down his face.

" How can I thank you ? " he said to Mr. Lethbridge.
" When everything looked so dark, and when I did not
know which way to turn—" He could not go on.

"'There's a silver lining to every cloud," said Kiss, " and
if it can be seen anywhere in this wilderness city it can be
seen here, in my friend Leth's house. I call a blessing upon
it. When you crossed this threshold you dropped on your
feet. But I told you how it would be. Now, Leth, perhaps
you would like to hear that, hearing I was out of an engagement, the manager of the Eden Theatre offered me
terms, but I have such faith in Linton's new piece that I
refused and kept myself open for it."

"I am perfectly satisfied," said Mr. Lethbridge.

"We can settle the affair at once, if you like," said
Kiss.

"Certainly, at once," assented Mr. Lethbridge.

" I brought the bill with me, and here it is on stamped
paper."

He produced it, and Mr. Lethbridge, reading it through,
accepted it, making it payable at the bank in which he had
for so long a time held a position of trust.

"Aunt Leth sent me to tell you," said Phœbe, popping in her head, "that tea is ready."

"Thank you, Phœbe," said Mr. Lethbridge; "come in. I want to introduce Mr. Linton to you."

How little did the bright and beautiful girl suspect that within the last few moments an awful and tragic thread had been woven into her life!

She entered the room, and looked timidly at the poor author.

" Not a word for me ? " said Kiss.

" Yes, Mr. Kiss," said Phœbe, giving him her hand.

" Mr. Linton—Phœbe," said her uncle Leth, encircling her waist with his arm. " This is my niece, Mr. Linton, whom I love as a daughter."

" Mr. Pamflett was speaking of you yesterday," said Mr. Linton.

" Mr. Pamflett ! " exclaimed Phœbe, shrinking at the name.

" Yes. He said you were the most lovely girl in all London, and that there was no service you could call upon him to render which he would not cheerfully perform."

"I scarcely know him, sir," murmured Phœbe.

"Let us go in to tea," said Mr. Lethbridge, "or mother will be impatient.   A terrible tyrant, Mr. Linton ; a terrible tyrant !"

CHAPTER XII.

IT was the merriest tea-party imaginable; and Aunt Leth's mind was at ease, in consequence of the time which had been afforded her to make suitable preparations for so eminent a guest as the dramatic author. In pouring out the tea, she helped him last, saying gaily,

"The first of the coffee, Mr. Linton, the last of the tea."

"A good homely saying," he observed. "I used to hear it from my mother. Though, really, I do not deserve such attention."

"Don't believe him, Aunt Leth," said Kiss. "Your dramatic author is as fond of the best as any common mortal."

The idea of comparing a dramatic author to a common mortal was certainly not to be lightly accepted by the young folk round the tea-table, who regarded Mr. Linton

11—2

as a being far above and removed from the general run of people. It was to them almost a surprise that he spoke and ate in exactly the same way as their other acquaintances; and out of the depths of their admiration, everything he did seemed to be invested with a certain superiority which raised him above his fellows. They cast timid and covert looks upon him, and noted his movements, so as to be able to give a faithful description of him, by-and-by, to their friends. It was fortunate for him that their observance was not too obtrusive, or it might have spoilt his appetite. As it was, he made an excellent tea, and tucked away the bread and butter and ham and eggs with a zest which delighted Aunt Leth. He declared that he had never tasted such tea, nor such eggs, nor such bacon, nor such bread and butter, nor such gooseberry jam; and, if appearances were to be trusted, and there was any value in words, never did mortal enjoy himself more than this poor author, who had been lifted from despair by the generous kindness of Uncle Leth. Kiss had imparted, hastily and confidentially, to Aunt Leth some particulars of Mr. Linton's circumstances, and had found time to descant upon his friend's virtues as a domestic man, of his love for his wife and children, and of his brave struggles against fortune. Aunt Leth's heart went out to Mr. Linton, and she said how proud she would be if he would bring his wife and little ones to see them. He replied that the honour would be on his side; but that, with his hostess's permission, he would wait until his new piece was produced at the Star Theatre. This temporizing reply was dictated by his sensitive spirit. He and his wife lived in two rooms, in a not very distinguished neighbourhood, and he was afraid of a return visit and its consequent humiliation. When his play was produced he would be able to remove to better quarters, and his wife would buy a new dress; then the acquaintanceship with this charming family could commence, and he would be in a position to return their hospitality.

"A new play!" exclaimed Aunt Leth. "Do you appear in it, Mr. Kiss?"

"Yes," said Kiss. "We hope to see you in the theatre on the first night. Uncle Leth has promised to supply each of you with a big stick, so that you may lead the applause."

"But there will be no getting in," said Aunt Leth.

"Linton will reserve a private box for you," said Kiss.

Eager heads turned to the poor author, eager eyes gazed at him.

"Madam," said Mr. Linton, " I shall be honoured if you will accept it. If you do not, I feel that my play will meet with failure."

"You are very good," said Aunt Leth. " We have never been to a first night, and have read so much about them. I am sure your play will be a great success; there can be no doubt of that."

The thoughts of Fanny and Phœbe instantly flew to the question of dress. A private box on a first night ! An event to be always remembered, especially with a play which was certain to be the talk of the town. It must be properly honoured.

"Mr. Linton has the manuscript of the play with him," said Kiss, "and if you have nothing better to occupy your time to-night I propose to read it to you, in order that you may form an opinion of it. What do you say ? "

What did they say?—there was a question ! If they had

nothing better to occupy their time ?—what *could* be better ? Why, the girls would be ready to throw over even a dance for such a treat ! They glowed with excitement, and Mr. Lethbridge, looking round upon the happy faces, was glad to think that he had signed the bill which Kiss had in his pocket at that moment, and which to-morrow would be in the possession of Jeremiah Pamflett.

" There's an audience for you," said Kiss to the author, pointing to the young people.

" A good augury," said the proud author. " I feel more hopeful than I have done for a long time past."

The females of the party presently left in a body to prepare the drawing-room for the promised reading, and then it was that Phœbe said to Aunt Leth :

" Oh, Aunt Leth, I have something to say, and I'm in that state of excitement that I'd better say it at once, before I forget it. Next Saturday is my birthday, you know."

" Yes, dear, I know," said Aunt Leth, giving the young girl a tender caress ; " and we shall keep it up by a little dance at home here. I intended to speak to you about it

night before you went to bed."

"You are so good to me, dear aunt," said Phœbe, "that I don't know how ever I can repay you. It would, I think, be impossible, whatever it might be in my power to do."

"My dear child," said Aunt Leth, "don't talk of repayment. You are as one of our own. What we do comes from our hearts. So you will manage to come here early on Saturday, and remain till Tuesday or Wednesday."

"No, aunt," said Phœbe, with many kisses, "I can't do that. You must all come to me."

"To you, dear! Where?"

"To Parksides, aunt."

Aunt Leth looked grave. "Have you your father's permission, Phœbe?"

"Yes, aunt; he gave it willingly. I don't mean to say it was his idea; it was mine, and he consented at once when I asked him. I can only ask you to a poor little tea," said Phœbe, her lips slightly trembling, "but I hope you won't mind. I should so like it! Uncle Leth and Fanny and Bob have never been to Parksides, and though I can't give them a grand entertainment, I don't think it will make any difference."

"Nothing can make any difference in our love for you, my dear."

"Then you *will* come, all of you!"

"Yes, dear, we will come, because I see it will be a pleasure to you, and that will make it a pleasure to us."

Aunt Leth pressed her hand fondly over the young girl's head, and just for one moment there were tears in both their eyes; but they were instantly dried, and with a smile and a kiss they busied themselves preparing for the reading of the play. These were soon completed, and the gentlemen were called in.

"Capital! capital!" exclaimed Kiss, as he contemplated the arrangements—the lights on the table, the chairs ranged round, the place of honour for himself so disposed that he could either sit or stand. "As good as a green-room, Linton."

"A great deal better," said the author, thinking of the various vain interests comprised in a company of actors, each listening to the lines of the character he was to play, and calling the piece good or bad according to the strength or weakness of that special part of it. He took his manuscript from his pocket and handed it to Kiss. The actor gazed with calm and impressive dignity at his audience. His movements were few and quiet and stately. He knew the value of repose. He was in his glory, master of the situation, and equal to the occasion. He opened the manuscript and was about to commence, when a diversion occurred. There was a sound at the door as of some person outside. Aunt Leth went to the door, opened it, glided into the passage, and returned.

"It is our servant," she whispered to Kiss. "She has heard of the reading, and implores to be allowed to be present. She is a very good girl. May she?"

"By all means," said Kiss. "A theatre is a packet of all sorts. Admit her."

In came 'Melia Jane, who, with awe on her features, seated herself at the back of the room, and fixed her eyes upon Kiss, who was to her a greater than Jove.

Then Kiss commenced in earnest, and quickly held his audience in thrall. He moved them to tears; he moved them to laughter. He so individualized each character, male and female, that there was no difficulty in following the course of the story. It contained tender and comic episodes, to which he gave full and distinctive weight, " bringing down the house," as he afterwards said, again and again. There was a song in the play, which he rendered amidst great applause; and as the author heard it, and saw the delighted appreciation of the little company, he hugged himself, as it were, and whispered inly : "It must be a success. It cannot, cannot fail!" Although the reading occupied two hours, there was not the least sign of weariness; and when it was finished, author and actor were overwhelmed with congratulations. As for 'Melia Jane, she so laughed, and cried, and clapped her hands, and stamped her feet, that the happy author, poor as he was, slyly slipped a shilling into her hand.

"It is," said Uncle Leth, "the very finest play that was ever written."

Upon this they were all agreed; and everyone prophesied a glorious success. Incidentally, Aunt Leth remarked, "And how beautifully you sang that song, Mr. Kiss?"

" Did I?" said Kiss. "Shall I sing you another?"

The proposal was received with clapping of hands; and

Kiss sang "Tom Bowline" with such tender effect that he was called upon for another.

"No," he said; "ask Linton. He knows a splendid song in another vein. Sing 'Little Billee,' Linton."

In the joy of his heart Mr. Linton could not refuse, and he began to sing Thackeray's "astonishing piece of nonsense." He had a thin quavering voice which suited the air; but somehow or other the song was not a success with this particular audience. Upon 'Melia Jane the effect was alarming. When the singer came to the lines,

> " There's little Bill is young and tender,
>   We're old and tough, so let's eat he,"

she slowly rose from her chair, with horror depicted on her face. The singer went on:

> " ' O Bill, we're going to kill and eat you,
>   So undo the collar of your chemie.'

> " When Bill received this infumation
>   He used his pocket-handkerchie.

> " ' O let me say my catechism,
>   As my poor mammy taught to me!' "

Here 'Melia Jane burst out blubbering so violently that she had to be conducted from the room. Mr. Linton concluded the song, however; but the applause which attended his effort was rather faint, and Kiss found it necessary to explain that the lines were really only nonsense lines. He himself soon restored the equilibrium by a sweet rendering of "Sally in our Alley"; and then followed other songs, by Phœbe and Fanny, and an old-fashioned duet by Aunt and Uncle Leth. Then there was a little bit of supper, at which Uncle Leth proposed the toast of "Success to Mr. Linton's delightful play," to which the author responded in feeling terms, and spoke of the happy evening he had spent. After actor and author were gone, Phœbe and the Lethbridges stopped up for an hour talking over the incidents of this remarkable night; but Uncle Leth said nothing of the bill for three hundred pounds to which he had put his name.

CHAPTER XIII.

CURL-PAPER CONFIDENCES.

WHEN two young women are closeted in their bedchamber after a pleasant day, and preparing for repose, then is the time for the interchange of sacred confidences. The events of the last few hours are touched upon with significant emphasis, the gentlemen are discussed and judged, and their personal peculiarities and excellencies commented upon with approval or otherwise. However quiet, demure, and comparatively unobservant the young ladies may have been, depend upon it not the smallest detail of the gentlemen's dress and manners has escaped their penetrating eyes. Especially is this the case upon the occasion of the introduction of a new male acquaintance. Everything appertaining to him is recalled, from the parting of his hair to the tying of his shoestrings. It would much astonish him to hear the pretty girls (all girls are pretty in their spring-time), who seemed to scarcely have courage to glance at him, speak of the colour of his eyes, of the cut of his clothes, of the quality of his moustache, of the size of his hands and feet, and the shape of his finger-nails. No learned judge in his summing up was ever so precise and correct, and the beauty or the despair of it is that these gossiping damsels are not only judges but juries, from whose verdict there is absolutely no appeal. Of course such sacred confidences are all the more interesting when the subjects for dissection are young unmarried men.

Many such conversations had Phœbe and Fanny held, and now, according to their wont, they proceeded to discuss the incidents of the evening, as they made their preparations for bed.

"I have often thought it a pity," said Phœbe, "that Mr. Kiss is not married."

"It *is* a pity," assented Fanny; "he is so good-natured and jolly that he deserves a good wife."

"And so clever," remarked Phœbe.

"And so good-looking. Phœbe, depend upon it, he has been crossed in love."

Phœbe sighed, and Fanny echoed the sigh. To these young hearts the very idea of being crossed in love was terribly sad.

"I *do* hope Mr. Linton's play will be a success," said Fanny, after a little pause. "Isn't it wonderful how a person can think of it all?"

"It is certain to be a success," said Phœbe, taking the last hair-pin out of her beautiful hair, which fell in waves over her shoulders.

Fanny gazed at her admiringly, and a charming picture indeed did the young girl present at that moment.

"If I envy you anything, Phœbe," said Fanny, "it is your hair. No one would think you had half as much."

"That's because it's so fine," said Phœbe, with a pleased smile.

"It's as fine as the finest silk," said Fanny, lifting bunches of it, and giving her cousin a quick affectionate kiss. "But you mustn't think I really envy you, Phœbe."

"I don't. I would change with you if I could."

"No, you wouldn't; no, you wouldn't," cried Fanny, with a merry laugh, "any more than I would with you."

" I am sure your hair is lovely, Fanny."

" It is altogether too coarse," said Fanny, with pretended pettishness. " But, there !—whoever gets me will have to make the best of it."

" Whoever gets you, Fanny, will have the dearest little wife in the world, and if he doesn't love every hair in your head he will be the most ungrateful of men—and I shall tell him so."

" I wonder who he will be," said Fanny, "and whether he knows that I've been growing up for him ? "

It was quite a natural remark for a light-hearted, innocent girl to make. Why, therefore, should it cause both the cousins to fall straightway into the mood ruminative—a mood which entails silence while it lasts.

" One thing I am determined upon," said Fanny, waking up, as it were ; " I won't have him unless he can waltz."

" If he can't," said Phœbe, with an arch smile, " you can teach him."

" Well, yes ; that *would* be nice." And Fanny, brush in hand, commenced to hum a favourite waltz, and took a few turns to it, saying, when she was again before the glass, "What were we speaking of, Phœbe, before my young man popped in?"

"About the play."

"We are all going on the first night—think of that! And in a private box—think of *that!* The observed of all observers, as Mr. Kiss would say. I shall feel so excited— almost as if I were the author—though such a thing is impossible."

"Why impossible, Fanny? You wrote a story when you were nine years old."

"Yes, and it commenced, "They were born in India without any father or mother." Was there anything ever so absurd?"

"The success of Mr. Linton's play will mean a great deal to him. He is not rich, I am afraid."

"If he isn't he ought to be," said Fanny, brushing with great care the tresses she pretended to despise; "wearing his brains out in the way he does. He *did* look anxious, didn't he, while Mr. Kiss was reading it? And how beautifully he read! I felt like kissing him when he was going through the love scenes. They *do* kiss a good deal on the stage, don't they ? "

"Yes," said Phœbe, speaking with difficulty, her mouth being full of hair-pins ; "but then they don't mean it."

Fanny made a face. " I shouldn't care for it that way," she said, and then she laughed, as though she had said something funny.

" Do you think Bob meant it," asked Phœbe, " when he said he was going to be an actor ? "

" Bob's a riddle," replied Fanny. " I give him up."

" He might do worse. It's quite a fashionable profession."

" It isn't a profession. Didn't Mr. Kiss tell us that an actor was a rogue and vagabond by Act of Parliament."

" That was only a joke. Mr. Kiss is a gentleman."

" Of course he is. The Prince of Wales once shook hands with him, and *he* wouldn't shake hands with any one *but* a gentleman. Do you wish you were a man, Phœbe ? "

" No."

" *I* do ! " said Fanny, with a decided nod of her head, the hair of which was by this time elaborately done up in curl-papers. Phœbe had also completed her preparations

12—2

for bed. "And now, Phœbe, let us have a chat." She made this proposition with a feminine obliviousness of having spoken a single word since she had locked the bedroom door.

"What about, Fanny?"

"Open your mouth and shut your eyes, and see what God will send you," said Fanny.

"Nonsense, Fanny."

"Very well—nonsense. Then we won't have a chat. Only"—and Fanny pursed up her lips and shook her paper-covered little head wisely.

"Only what?"

"That you'll be sorry for it—that's all."

"What a tease you are! There!" Phœbe opened her mouth and shut her eyes.

"Don't move—don't stir!" cried Fanny, and she took from her dress an envelope, the edge of which she placed between Phœbe's teeth. "What is this?"

"A piece of paper. I'd sooner have a chocolate cream."

"You would, eh? Well, here's your chocolate cream—

here's a packet of them—and if I don't tell him when he comes home, my name isn't Fanny Lethbridge."

This remark caused Phœbe to open her eyes very quickly, and the colour on her face to come and go. Fanny's right hand was behind her back.

" Tell whom, Fanny ? "

" ' Tell whom, Fanny ? ' " mimicked Fanny. " Now *is* there more than one Frederick Cornwall, Esq., in the world ? "

" There may be—in the London Directory."

" But they don't all write letters from Switzerland to Camden Town, do they ? "

" Have you received another letter from Mr. Cornwall, Fanny ? "

" Yes, I have ; and here it is. It came this morning."

" And you kept it to yourself all this time ! "

" How could I show it to you before? You had hardly been in the house two minutes when papa came home with Mr. Kiss and Mr. Linton. Then there was Bob hanging about, and you know how he scowls when I speak lovingly· of Fred—I beg his pardon, Mr. Frederick Cornwall. Then there was helping mother with the tea. Then there was the reading of the play. Then there were the songs. With all that excitement, the letter went clean out of my head—except that I thought you would like it all the better if we read it together quietly here, where nobody can disturb us."

"You are a dear, good girl!"

"Of course I am, and you're another." Whereupon the cousins, with their arms round each other's necks, fondly embraced. They were sitting now on the bed very cosily, side by side. "Phœbe, I have something very horrifying to tell you."

"He hasn't met with an accident—he isn't ill?" exclaimed Phœbe, turning pale.

"Not a bit of it. He is as well as five feet eleven, aged six-and-twenty, should be. No, it isn't that; but it is about him, though."

"Tell me, Fanny."

"For a long time I have had my suspicions, but I wouldn't venture to breathe them to you. I watched mamma; I watched papa. When we were talking of him—it was always I who brought up his name—I set traps for them, and they fell into them unsuspiciously. And then there was what mamma said, in a pretended off-hand way, this morning, when she gave me the letter from Fred. It amounts to this, Phœbe "—she dropped her voice, and said in a whisper—"they think he comes after *me !* "

" Why shouldn't he, dear ? "

" Why should he, dear ? "

Phœbe stroked her cousin's face fondly, and rested her head on Fanny's shoulder.

" I hope," said Fanny, " that they won't be disappointed when they find out that he doesn't mean *me,* after all. But I don't think they will be when they know it is you, darling."

" Oh, Fanny ! And he has never said one word to me !"

" What of that, sly puss ? I can speak with my eyes quite as well as I can with my tongue ; and Fred Cornwall is a great deal cleverer than I am. I don't positively hate him, you know."

" It would be very wrong of you to do so."

" And I don't positively love him. I like him, just a little, in a so-soish way. How it might have been if I didn't happen to have the dearest, sweetest, prettiest cousin that a foolish girl could ever boast of, isn't for me to say." (More hugs and embraces here.) " I *might* have fallen a victim to his lordship's charms ; I don't say I should, but I might."

" But, Fanny," said Phœbe, in a low tone, her lips slightly trembling, " it is foolish, it is wrong, to speak like this."

" Now, Phœbe ! " said Fanny, holding up a warning fore-finger.

" Well, I won't say a word."

" That's a good, sensible, sweet-hearted cousin."

" You are not sorry, Fanny ? "

" That he is not made for me ? Well, it gives me a pang here to say no "—she placed her hand on her heart, and emitted a comically pathetic sigh—"because, you know, he *is* the very loveliest waltzer that ever put his arm round a girl's waist. You said so yourself. Now confess, Phœbe, if Fred *did*—eh ?—you wouldn't run away, would you ? " Phœbe's silence was the most eloquent answer she could give to her cousin's question, which, enigmatical as it may sound in the ears of unsentimental persons, was as clear and as sweet to the young girls as the sound of wedding bells.

"If he doesn't," added Fanny, energetically, "I shall call him out!"

"Would Aunt and Uncle Leth be very angry?" murmured Phœbe.

"Why, Phœbe," replied Fanny, reproachfully, "they love you as much as they love me. I should feel dreadful if I wasn't sure of that. We are more than cousins, dear; we are sisters. Just put your ear to my heart: don't you hear it beat, 'Phœbe, Phœbe'? It is a good job for Fred Cornwall that I am *not* a man. *He* shouldn't have you, if I were; no—not if he were fifty Fred Cornwalls. I would run away with you, just as Young Lochinvar did with—I forget her name, but it doesn't matter; I'd do it. Isn't it strange that elderly people can't see half as well as young?—they don't look at what is under their noses; they are always looking over their spectacles."

"Aunt and Uncle Leth don't wear them," said Phœbe smiling.

"I am speaking—metaphorically. That's not my word; it's Fred's—rather a favourite with him, you know. Of course, if they asked me plainly, I should tell them; but it wouldn't do for me to start it—would it?—till things are properly settled. They will be overjoyed, Phœbe; and so shall I be; for, don't you see, my dear, when you are disposed of, there will be a chance for *me*, and if a young gentleman comes to the house there will be no mistake the next time, because I shall be the only disposable young lady in view. To that young gentleman, whoever he is, wherever he may be, I extend an invitation—I say, with a courtesy, 'Come!' Oh! but I must tell you, Phœbe, it was so funny. You remember the last time Fred Cornwall had tea with us here—before he went on his holiday trip?"

"Yes."

"*I* invited him, and perhaps you may remember that I wrote to you and told you to be sure and come and spend two or three days with us. I didn't mention Fred's name in my letter to you, for you would have kept away." It was delightful to hear Fanny's laugh at this innocent badinage. "Well, you came—and Fred came—and I sent Bob off to the theatre, with an order. Now what does mamma pride herself especially upon in the way of jams?"

" Her gooseberry jam."

" Yes, and it really is very fine ; I never tasted any half as good. Well, all the while we were at tea I saw it was you Fred was feeding on."

" Fanny, Fanny ! You are incorrigible ! "

"Am I ? Nevertheless, I am right. When he wasn't looking at you, he was thinking of you ; when he wasn't thinking of you, he was looking at you. I am quite an experienced person in love matters. ' Mr. Cornwall,' said mamma, ' this is home-made gooseberry jam—my own making. What do you think of it ?' ' It is a dream,' replied Fred. He was gazing at you when he passed that very remarkable opinion upon mamma's gooseberry jam. Afterward I heard mamma say to papa, ' Did you hear what Mr. Cornwall said of my gooseberry jam ? He said it was a dream. Depend upon it, he means something by it.' And I happening to pop into the room just then, mamma looked at papa significantly ; and papa looked at mamma significantly ; and then both of them kissed me. I couldn't help laughing to myself and thinking, ' Mamma will have to try her gooseberry jam on some other young man.' And now, Phœbe, we will read Fred's letter."

" How is it, Fanny, that Mr. Cornwall has written you so many letters ? " asked Phœbe.

" Jealous ? " inquired Fanny.

" No, I have no right to be ; Mr. Cornwall is really nothing to me."

" You should have ended that sentence with 'yet.' ' Mr. Cornwall is really nothing to me—yet !' Quite right for you to call him *Mr.* Cornwall ; I shall call him Fred, to his face. He will like it—so shall I."

" How you rattle on, Fanny !"

" Yes," said Fanny, composedly ; " papa used to call me a regular little chatterbox."

" You have not answered my question, Fanny."

" Oh, about the letters. How is it Fred has written me so many ? I have received one, two, three, and this is the fourth. A famous correspondence, isn't it ? The fact is," said Fanny unblushingly, " I asked him to write to me, and he, being such a polite young fellow, couldn't very well refuse. I did it quite openly; mamma was present. 'You might write me a nice chatty letter or two, Mr. Cornwall,' said I, ' while you are away.' ' I shall be very happy,' said he, looking at mamma, 'if I may be allowed.' '*I* have no objection,' said mamma. His asking mamma was almost like a declaration, wasn't it? Many a man has been had up for breach of promise for less than that. And to think of a lawyer so committing himself! But I don't believe they are a bit cleverer than other people ; they only pretend to be. 'But I shall stipulate,' said Fred, 'that you answer my letters.' ' Of course I will,' said I, without asking mamma ; and I have. In the last one I wrote to him I said that you sent him your dearest love."

"I hope you did not say that, Fanny."

"If I didn't, I meant it ; so that it amounts to the same thing. Don't be ungrateful, Phœbe. I inveigled him into writing to me for your sake, not for mine, though I *do* wear his letters next to my heart. He is supposed to be address-ing me in his correspondence, but he is really writing to you, and he knows that you read every word. Is there one of his letters without a lot about you in it?"

"He is always thoughtful."

"A model young man ; when he comes home we'll put him in a glass case. And now we must really get to sleep, or we shall have mamma crying outside in the passage, 'Girls, girls, put out the light!' Don't you feel tired, Phœbe?"

"But the letter, Fanny!"

"Oh, the letter! Well, if I wasn't almost forgetting it! I suppose it *must* be read. See, it is addressed from the Grimsel Hospice. That's where the monks are. What a splendid monk Fred would make! He really ought to become one. What do *you* think, Phœbe?"

Then Fanny kissed her cousin half a dozen times, and proceeded to read Fred Cornwall's letter.

CHAPTER XIV.

A BIT OF EDELWEISS.

" My dear Miss Lethbridge—"

("That's altogether too formal, isn't it?" said Fanny, looking up from the letter. "Why doesn't the stupid fellow commence with, 'My own dearest Fanny'? It would be very much nicer, wouldn't it?")

" My dear Miss Lethbridge,—Since my last we have had glorious weather, and I have been to no end of places, enjoying myself thoroughly. The only drawback is that I am without a companion, and that I sometimes feel rather lonely—"

("If there ever *was* a young fellow," said Fanny, "cut out for a family man, it is Fred.")

" And that I sometimes feel rather lonely. But we cannot have everything we wish for in this world, and I shall soon be home. One satisfaction is that I am making myself well acquainted with the route I have taken—as delightful a track as can be imagined—and that it will be a great pleasure by-and-by to guide some one who has never been to the beauty-land of Switzerland over the ground I have traversed—"

("I wonder," said Fanny, "if he has anybody in his eye, and whether he is thinking of a honeymoon!")

"Over the ground I have traversed. I received your pleasant, chatty letter, telling me all the news, and I cannot thank you enough for it. You are a model of a correspondent. So you all went to hear *Faust* at Covent Garden; I can imagine how you enjoyed yourselves, loving music as you do. When I was at Milan I went to La Scala, about which everybody who hasn't seen it raves. It isn't a patch on Covent Garden. You say it would have done my heart good if I had seen how beautiful Miss Farebrother looked—"

("I gave him," said Fanny, "a most elaborate description of our dresses.")

"To see how beautiful Miss Farebrother looked. You need scarcely have told me that; she always looks beautiful —and so do you—"

("*I* come in," said Fanny, tossing her head, "as a kind of make-weight. Out of common politeness he could not have said less.")

"And so do you. On my way to the Grimsel this afternoon I stopped at Handek to see the Falls. I am not sure that I do not admire them more than any I have yet passed. They are truly grand; and I wish I could have gathered some of the wonderful ferns low down the ravine to have inclosed in this letter. Before I reached the Falls I stopped at a hut, and there was a girl shelling peas. Quite a young girl, not more than seventeen, I should say; but there was something about her that reminded me of Miss Farebrother. Nothing like so pretty and sweet; but her hair was the same colour, and she was about the same height. She got me some milk, and I stopped a few minutes to rest, and helped her to pick her peas—"

("It has been my opinion," said Fanny, "ever since I had the pleasure of Fred's acquaintance, that he was little better than a flirt. He ought to be ashamed of himself. The least he could do was to keep these things to himself.")

"Helped her to pick her peas. We had an agreeable

chat, although she spoke a patois of which I did not understand a single word. It was very comical—"

("Very," said Fanny, with a fine touch of sarcasm.)

"Comical. Then I went on my way rejoicing, and it was quite dark when I reached the Grimsel. The monks are very hospitable; they gave me a good dinner and a good bottle of wine, for which they charge nothing; only one is expected to put something in the box for the poor before he leaves the hospice. I am up here in the mountains, nearly seven thousand feet above the level of the sea; out side there is a melancholy, sombre sheet of water called the Todten-See, or the Dead Lake. It is said to contain no living thing, only ghosts. Before I go to bed I shall go and see them. I am sorry to hear that the firm in which Bob was employed has failed, and that he is out of a situation. Hope he will soon get another, and that his career will shed lustre and renown on the name of Lethbridge. And I am truly sorry to hear that Miss Farebrother has sprained her wrist—"

("Oh, Fanny!" cried Phœbe, "I didn't." "I told him you did," said Fanny, calmly. "When a man is away, things must *not* be allowed to languish. The interest *must* be kept up somehow.")

"Sprained her wrist. She must take the greatest care of it. Of course you do not allow her to touch the piano. You ask me how she would look with her hair cut short—"

("Well!" gasped Phœbe. "It is really too bad of you.. Nothing could induce me to have my hair cut off. I have never mentioned such a thing." "*I* mentioned it," said Fanny, with a little laugh. "Trust me for managing these affairs. He will be overjoyed when he comes home and finds your hair just as beautiful as when he left. He will say something about it, to which you will reply—exposing me, of course—and then he will pay you no end of compliments.")

"With her hair cut short. Are you serious? I know what a quiz you are, and I suspect you are amusing yourself at my expense. I can hardly believe that Miss Farebrother has any such intention. I never saw such beautiful hair as hers—"

("Thank you, sir," said Fanny.)

"Such beautiful hair as hers, and she will be doing very

13—2

wrong if she allows herself to be persuaded to adopt what I
consider an odious fashion.   You know my opinion about
mannish women; I would banish them to some distant
island if I had my way, where, as there would be no men
among them, there might be a chance of their recovering
their right senses.   When I was in Milan I bought three
lace handkerchiefs: one for Miss Farebrother, one for
yourself, and one for your kind mother.   I have something
also for Uncle Leth and Bob.   Please give them all my
very kindest regards, and tell Aunt Leth I am longing to
have tea with her, and to taste her wonderful gooseberry
jam again."

(Fanny had to stop here to laugh, and then she said:
" Look, Phœbe, here are a lot of dots.   His recollection of
the gooseberry jam overcame him, and he went out to the
Dead Lake to see the ghosts.")

" I threw down my pen, and went out for a stroll.   It is
a beautiful night.   The Dead Lake does not sustain its
reputation when the stars are shining on it.   I tried to
conjure up the ghosts, but they would not come.   Instead
of ghosts, all sorts of pleasant memories took shape, for the

chief of which I have to thank your happy home. I thought of you all, and of the many acts of hospitality for which I am indebted to you. There is in such scenes as this a spirit of peace inexpressibly soothing, forming a reminiscence to be long remembered. The reflection of the stars in the still waters rendered it impossible to credit their evil reputation. The lake was a fairy lake, and as such I shall always think of it. Upon entering the hospice I heard the monks praying in low voices. Now I must to bed. Convey my kindest remembrances to Miss Fare-brother, and receive the same yourself, from

" Yours very sincerely,

FREDERICK CORNWALL."

" That is something like a letter," said Fanny. " Fred is quite a poet. Don't you think so ? "

" He writes beautifully," replied Phœbe.

" Lace handkerchiefs," said Fanny. "I wonder whose will be the prettiest ? Mine, I should say."

" You deserve the best."

" There can be no doubt of that; but then men are so

ungrateful.   I must confess I can't quite get over that girl at Handek.   The idea of his helping her to shell peas!"

"It was very kind of him."

"It was nothing of the sort; it was a downright shameless piece of flirtation, and I shall take him to task for it. I shouldn't so much have minded it if *I* had been the girl; would you?   Oh, how foolish of me!—there is a postscript to the letter.   Just think of a young woman forgetting a 'P.S.'!"

"As if you did not know it was there!" said Phœbe, with a tender smile.   "What does it say?"

"Well, I never!   Just listen.   'P.S.—My own dearest girl—'"

"Eh?" cried Phœbe.

"No; it is a mistake of mine.   He has left that out. 'P.S.—I have kept this letter by me four days, and it is time I posted it, or I shall be home before you receive it. I expect to reach London on Friday morning.'   What do you think of that, Phœbe?   How many to the minute is your heart going?   Friday morning.   The day after to-morrow.   I shan't be able to sleep a wink.   But there is something more, Phœbe; that is not the end of the post-script. It goes on : ' Enclosed are two small packets, one with your name outside, one with Miss Farebrother's. I dare say you have not seen the flower they contain. It is the edelweiss, a flower which, always worn, brings luck and good fortune. If you will give me the opportunity, when I come home, I shall regard it as a great favour if you will allow me to put a piece of edelweiss in lockets for you both. With constant regards, Fred C.' Here is your packet, Phœbe."

Phœbe opened the paper, and gazed at the white flower, around which the traveller had arranged a few forget-me-nots.

" He calls it," said Fanny, " a flower of luck and good fortune. *I* know the right name for it, if he doesn't."

" What is its right name ? " asked Phœbe.

" It is a love flower—nothing less. I shall put mine under my pillow, and shall dream of My Own. Not yours —mine; I am not a poacher. I will tell you what he is like in the morning. Good-night, dear Phœbe."

" Good-night, darling," said Phœbe.

Both the girls put their flowers of love under their pillows, and had happy dreams.

CHAPTER XV.

No more chivalrous knight than Tom Barley ever drew breath, but notwithstanding his devotion to Phœbe, certain incontrovertible conclusions had for some time past forced themselves upon him. A number of men live to eat; a much larger number eat to live. Without reference to his inclinations, Tom Barley's circumstances did not enable him to do the former, and he found it exceedingly hard to do the latter. Between him and Mrs. Pamflett existed an unconquerable antipathy. Being of an independent order of mind, he was barely civil to her; and, as she kept the key of the cupboard, she repaid him in full by either throwing food to him as she would to a dog, or giving him none at all. She tolerated him because he was useful to her in the way of chopping wood and doing various odd jobs of a rough nature; but for this, she would long ago have had him dismissed. Her son Jeremiah, who came regularly to Parksides on Miser Farebrother's business, never failed to put a spoke in Tom's wheel as he termed it ; but his mother was successful in mollifying him by recounting the hardships to which Tom had to submit.

"He's little better than starved," she said to her son, "and he hasn't a rag to his back."

"Serve him right," growled Jeremiah ; "I'd like to see him hanged ! "

He never forgot the beating he had received in the village, by the instigation of Tom Barley, on the occasion of his first visit to Parksides ; and with him, never to forget was never to forgive. With prudent care of his bones he steered clear of a collision with Tom, who was strong enough to tackle half a dozen men such as he ; but he would gladly have seized an opportunity to do Tom an ill turn. Tom, the least vindictive being that ever wore rags, had forgotten the incident years ago, and would have met with civility any advances which Jeremiah might have made to him ; but as Miser Farebrother's managing clerk invariably scowled at him when they happened to meet, he took refuge in silence and avoidance. Jeremiah had made great strides since he first entered the miser's service. He had mastered the intricacies and the rogueries of the money-lending business, and was the sharpest of sharp knaves —without feeling, without a heart, intent only upon his own interests and the gratification of his own pleasures. It has already been shown that he was lending money upon his own account ; but this was done without the cognizance of the miser, who would have strongly resented such an encroach-ment upon his domain. Miser Farebrother would have found it difficult—indeed, almost impossible—to get along now without Jeremiah ; the constant cramp in his bones, which had kept him so frequently and for so long a time together a prisoner in Parksides, grew worse instead of better, and Jeremiah had taken the fullest advantage which these absences had offered to him. There were matters of business which Jeremiah, and Jeremiah alone, could explain : sums of money were owing which, without Jeremiah, could never have been recovered ; certain of the questionable transactions by means of which Miser Fare-brother had amassed wealth were entered and recorded in a manner so peculiar that Jeremiah and no other person understood them. He had played his cards apparently well. The question to be decided was, where the game was going to lead him.

On the Friday upon which Fred Cornwall was expected home, two or three pregnant circumstances took place affecting our heroine. It was the day previous to her birthday, on which she had obtained her father's consent to the visit of the Lethbridges to Parksides. Phœbe had returned home on Thursday evening, intent upon making preparations for the visit of her dearest friends. Before she left Camden Town a little conversation took place between her and her aunt with respect to this birthday celebration.

"You must not expect much," Phœbe said; "I cannot afford to do as I would wish."

"Whatever it is," said Aunt Leth, "it will be as welcome as the best. I should say, a cup of tea and some nice thin bread and butter."

"Yes," said poor Phœbe; "that will be all, I am afraid."

"But even that," said Aunt Leth, "will entail a small expense. Let me see your purse."

"No, aunt; it is all right; and I must go at once."

"There is no hurry, my dear; you have at least half an hour to spare. Fanny is going with you to the station, and she will not be ready for the next twenty minutes. Show me your purse, Phœbe."·

"Aunt dear—"

"My dear child, I insist, or I shall think you do not love me."

Phœbe's purse was out in a moment; but she repented when it was in Aunt Leth's hand.

"You foolish girl!" said Aunt Leth, looking into the purse, and pinching Phœbe's cheek; "there is next to nothing in it. Come, now—it is too late, I hope, for secrets between us—tell me all."

Phœbe, in a low voice, told of the conversation between her father and herself, and of his giving her a florin for a birthday present. Aunt Leth did not look grave as she listened; on the contrary, she nodded and smiled brightly. It was not in her nature to do the slightest thing to aggravate the gloomy surroundings of the young girl's home. Her heart was filled with sweet pity for her niece's lot, and it was for her to shed light on Phœbe's life.

"My dear child," she said, "do you look upon me as a mother?"

"Indeed I do, dear aunt."

"Would you wish to vex me?"

"No, aunt; no."

"Then you must let me have my way. I know what is right and what is best. I have a little treasure-box, which I find very useful often when I am in a wilful mood. It is sometimes filled with saved pennies, and you have no idea how they mount up. Don't oppose me, Phœbe, or I will not kiss you." In proof of which she gave her niece a number of affectionate kisses at once. "I am going to my treasure-box now."

She produced it from her desk, and put fifteen shillings into Phœbe's purse. Then she closed the purse, and pressed it into the girl's hand.

"What can I say, aunt?" murmured Phœbe, her eyes filled with tears.

"Say, my dear, 'I am glad my aunt treats me as she would treat her own child.' I have served you just as I would serve Fanny."

" I shall never be able to repay you, dear aunt."

" You are repaying me, Phœbe, every day of your life."

The gratitude which filled Phœbe's heart had something sacred in it. But, indeed, that happy house was more than a home to the young girl—it was a sanctuary.

Therefore Phœbe, unloved and neglected as she was in Parksides, was perfectly happy on the day before her birthday. She would be able to make her tea-table quite gay, and she went to the village and laid out to great advantage the money her aunt had put in her purse.

" Good afternoon, Miss Phœbe."

It was Jeremiah Pamflett who accosted her. He was on a visit to the miser, with books and papers under his arm.

"Good afternoon," said Phœbe, who was also carrying parcels. She would have hurried on and left him, after these salutations, but he was too quick for her.

" Won't you shake hands with me, Miss Phœbe ? "

" I can't ; they are full."

" Where there's a will there's a way. You had better shake hands with me, or your father will be angry when I tell him."

This threat served him. Phœbe managed to extend her hand, which he took and held in his for a longer time than was necessary.

"What a pretty hand you have, Miss Phœbe ? "

She shrank at the compliment, and snatched her hand from his grasp. He did not take umbrage at this action, pretending not to notice it.

" We are both going home, Miss Phœbe. May I offer you my arm ? "

" I can do quite well without, thank you," said Phœbe.

" And as well with. I always like to be polite to ladies ; a gentleman can't do less. Let me carry a parcel or two for you. I shall tell your father that I assisted you, and he will be pleased. I do all his business for him, you know, and he has the greatest confidence in me. I do all I can to deserve it, I am sure. Thank you. Don't you feel more comfortable now ? I should if I was a young lady, and a gentleman had insisted upon helping me."

Had it not been that she was fearful of angering her father, Phœbe would on no account have accepted his assistance; but he forced it upon her, and compelled her to take his arm. He walked proudly through the village with his lovely charge, tilting his hat a little on one side of his head to show his quality. Sometimes he dropped one of Phœbe's parcels, and when she once stooped to pick it up and their heads touched, he became quite merry, and asked her which was the hardest. She spoke scarcely a word; but he beguiled the way with anecdote and jest, and, when they reached Parksides, declared it was the pleasantest walk he had ever taken. She ran up to her room and left him alone. For himself, though he was at the door of the house, he did not enter it; he turned back, and walked about the grounds in thought, saying more than once to himself, "Upon my soul it wouldn't be half a bad move!" emphasizing his remark by slapping his leg smartly. On his way back to the house he encountered Tom Barley, and, elated by his reflections, he cried out:

"Hallo, you beggar ! How are *you* getting on ? Making your fortune ? "

"No," said Tom Barley ; " are you ?"

" Yes," said Jeremiah, exultantly. " *I'm* getting on like a house on fire. Here's a penny—no, a ha'penny for you."

Tom Barley threw it back savagely, and it grazed Jeremiah's forehead.

"I could have you up for that," said Jeremiah, edging away from Tom. "Assault and battery, you know. If you give me any of your cheek I'll land you at the station-house."

"Give me any of yours," retorted Tom, "and I'll break every bone in your body !"

Jeremiah deemed it best to walk away, which he did rather swiftly, and with decided nervousness. Upon making his appearance before his mother he worked himself up into a great passion, and said that Tom Barley had set upon him with a knife, and had threatened his life. She soothed him, and advised him to inform Miser Farebrother, which he promised to do; and being further mollified by a draught of ale and a plate of cold meat and pickles, he condescended to be in a better humour.

"You haven't kissed me, Jeremiah," said Mrs. Pamflett.

" Oh, bother ! " he said, brushing her cheek with his lips. "I like to kiss girls. I say, mother, how pretty Phœbe's grown ! "

" Miss Farebrother?" asked his mother, somewhat startled.

" I said ' Phœbe,' didn't I ? She's about as pretty as they make 'em. I met her in the village, and she took my arm. A little stuck-up at first, but I soon brought her to her senses. Mother, what do you think of me ? "

" You are the best son in the world," she replied, readily, " and the cleverest man in England."

" Yes, I think I can show them a trick or two. Are you proud of me, mother ? "

" Indeed I am, Jeremiah ? "

" Am I a handsome man, mother ? '

" A handsomer couldn't be found, Jeremiah."

" Am I good enough for any girl ? "

" Indeed you are. She'll be a lucky girl you set your heart on, my boy."

" Oh, come, now ! I don't know so much about hearts. I know which side I want my bread buttered—eh, mother ? "

14—2

"Certainly, Jeremiah."

" Well, then, why shouldn't it be ? "

" Why shouldn't what be ? " asked Mrs. Pamflett, very much mystified.

Jeremiah put his forefinger to the side of his nose. " When I tell you, mother, you'll be as wise as I am."

" But do tell me, Jeremiah," the fond mother pleaded.

"Still tongue, wise head," said he. " No ; I'll have a good think over it first."

He went up to Miser Farebrother with his books and papers, and when the interview was over he returned to his mother, who by that time had a hot meal prepared for him. Before she dished it up he asked her whether she could find Tom Barley.

"The old skinflint wants to see him," said Jeremiah, with an upward jerk of his head, in the direction of the room occupied by Miser Farebrother. " He has something very particular to say to the beggar, which will open his eyes a bit. Go and find him, mother, and send him up. I'll wait. Pleasure first, business afterward."

Tom Barley happened to be within hail, and Mrs. Pam-flett sent him up to the miser, and then attended to her son. She waited till he was well primed, and presumably therefore in a more complaisant humour, and then she said, coaxingly, " Won't you tell me, Jeremiah, what you meant by saying ' Why shouldn't it be ? ' "

" No, I won't, and that's flat," replied Jeremiah ; " at least, I won't till I've a mind to. But Phœbe *is* a pretty girl, isn't she, mother ? "

" I was pretty once," sighed Mrs. Pamflett.

" Shouldn't have thought it. But women go off so. I don't know that I've ever seen a much prettier girl than Phœbe."

Mrs. Pamflett opened her eyes wide ; she began to have a glimmering of her son's meaning.

" There's styles," continued Jeremiah. " Some like one style, some like another. For my part, I'm not particular, so long as a girl's nice looking. It don't matter to me much whether they're dark or fair, or long or short, so long as they're that. Mother, you're not a bad sort, and I'll be open with you."

"You're my own boy!" exclaimed the fond mother, pressing her son's head to her bosom.

"I wish you wouldn't!" cried Jeremiah. "I don't care to have your buttons grinding into my nose. When you've recovered yourself, perhaps you'll sit down."

Mrs. Pamflett obeyed meekly, murmuring, "I couldn't help it, Jeremiah."

"Well, do help it. I tell you once for all, do help it. I don't want to have my nose skinned. I've a good mind now not to tell you."

"Do tell me, Jeremiah," implored Mrs. Pamflett—"do! And I'll never take you sudden again."

"Very well, then; but mind you keep your word. You're always at it, hugging and pressing me as if I was a bit of wood! Yes; I say there's styles, and what I say on the top of that is that I ain't particular so long as everything else is O.K."

"What's O.K.?" inquired Mrs. Pamflett, anxiously.

"All correct, of course. You don't know much, and that's a fact. Trust me for seeing to things being right. You would have to get up very early in the morning to get ahead of *me*. Now don't exasperate me by asking too many questions. Everything in time, so don't you be in a hurry. A spider ain't, when he's got a bluebottle in his web. Take a lesson from him."

" I will, Jeremiah," said Mrs. Pamflett, humbly; "but who's the bluebottle, and who's the spider ? "

" There you are, asking questions again. You rile a fellow, that's what you do. Mother, what do you think of Phœbe ? "

" I don't think much of her," replied Mrs. Pamflett, shortly. She would not have answered so candidly had she not been taken off her guard. Her opinion of Phœbe, however, did not seem to disturb Jeremiah, who said :

"Women never hit it, somehow. Is she proud ? "

" Yes."

" I thought she was ; but if any man can bring her to book, I can. Does she sauce you ? "

" She seldom speaks to me."

" Women are the crookedest creatures going ; they never answer straight. Does she sauce you ? "

"No."

"Has she got a sweetheart?"

"Not that I know of."

"Does she receive letters?"

"Only from her relations in Camden Town."

"Mr. and Mrs. Lethbridge," said Jeremiah, chuckling, and feeling his pocket, in which an acceptance for three hundred pounds with Mr. Lethbridge's name to it was safely secured. "I know something of *them*. Do you think she's in love?"

"No."

"It wouldn't matter if she was." And here Jeremiah paused, and gave himself up to thought, with his fingers stretched across his brows. Mrs. Pamflett observed him earnestly, but did not disturb him. "Mother, would you like to see me ride in my carriage—my own carriage?"

"I should be the proudest woman in England, Jeremiah —my own Jeremiah!"

"Stow that!" cried Jeremiah, holding her off. "No more buttons! You'd like to see me ride in my carriage, would you? There are more unlikely things. You said

I was good enough for any girl. Am I good enough for Phœbe?"

" A million times too good, my boy," said Mrs. Pamfle:t, enthusiastically.

"That's a blessing. She ought to be grateful. When I met her in the village she had a lot of parcels. Does she go shopping for you?"

"Not she. Perhaps she's been buying some things for her birthday. She's going to give her aunt and uncle tea here."

"Oho! And when *is* Phœbe's birthday, mother?"

"To-morrow."

Jeremiah grinned, his eyes glittered. " I'm in luck's way," he said. "And now, mother, give me a glass of brandy and water, and I'll cut my lucky."

"When shall I see you again, Jeremiah?" she asked, after mixing the beverage, which he tossed off with a relish.

" Sooner than you expect. Oh, well, I don't mind telling you. I'm coming here to-morrow to wish Phœbe many happy returns. Ta-ta! Well, if you must kiss me—there you are, hugging me again! Why can't you do it gently?"

CHAPTER XVI.

TOM BARLEY HAS A SCENE WITH THE MISER.

MEANWHILE Miser Farebrother and Tom Barley were "having it out" upstairs in the miser's room. Jeremiah Pamflett had put a very strong case before Miser Farebrother. He said that every time he came down to Parksides, Tom Barley laid wait for him and threatened to take his life.

"It's no fault of mine," said Jeremiah, "that I'm not as strong as that hulking vagabond, who makes any amount of money by robbing you. If you like to be robbed, I've nothing to say to it. Nobody loses anything but yourself. But I can't be coming regularly down here in fear of my life. You couldn't expect me to."

In short, Jeremiah indirectly gave Miser Farebrother to understand that if he retained Tom Barley in his employ he would have to come more often to London to look

through the books and papers; and that he, Jeremiah Pamflett, would have to come less often to Parksides. Jeremiah
was cunning enough to know that he was on safe ground in
making this declaration. He had felt his way before he
had arrived at it, and the miser was furious. It was impossible for him to go more often to London; there was no
one he could trust but Jeremiah, and, in the light of a
possible rupture, he placed an exaggerated value upon his
clerk's services.

"He drew a knife upon me," said Jeremiah, "as I was
coming here, because he saw me escorting Miss Farebrother
home. She was in the village making purchases, and I
thought it my duty to protect her."

"Quite right, quite right," said Miser Farebrother. "She
ought to be much obliged to you."

"She was," said Jeremiah.

"Making purchases, eh?" exclaimed Miser Farebrother.
"What was she purchasing—eh? You don't know? What's
that you say? Oh, Tom Barley! I'll soon settle with him.
They all rob me—everybody, everybody! You are the only
one I can trust—the only one, the only one!"

" There's nothing I wouldn't do for you," said Jeremiah, fervently. " I'd work my fingers off—"

" There, there !" said Miser Farebrother, fretfully. " Don't make protestations. I hate them. It is your interest to do your duty. I pay you well for it."

" You do ; and I am grateful," said Jeremiah, feeling in his heart as if he would like to strangle his master. " But you don't care for that sort of thing, and I'll not say any-thing more."

" No ; don't, don't !" groaned the miser. " Go ; and send Tom Barley up to me."

Jeremiah nodded, and went out of the room. Miser Farebrother's eyes followed him ; and when the door was closed, he groaned :

" He's as bad as the rest, I believe ; but I've not been able to find him out. Is he cunninger and cleverer than I am ? Curse my bones ! Why can't I buy a new set ? There isn't an honest man in the whole world. If Phœbe had been a boy instead of a girl, I might have had a little peace of mind ; but as it is, I'm robbed right and left—

right and left! Who's that at the door? Come in, can't you? Oh, it's you, Tom Barley?"

"Yes, it's me," said Tom. "What do you want of me?"

"Speak respectfully," screamed the miser.

"I am, though I've got no particular call to," said Tom. Truth to tell he was not in an amiable temper, what with his hunger, and his rags, and his meeting with Jeremiah. "You sent for me. What do you want? And mind this —I don't stir hand or foot till I get something to eat."

Miser Farebrother became suddenly quite cool. It was generally the case when an antagonist he had in his power was before him.

"Something to eat, eh? You scoundrel! you have the stomach of an ostrich."

"I wish I had," said Tom; "then I could fill it with stones and rusty nails. As it is, I can't get those things down. I give you warning—"

"What!" cried Miser Farebrother; "you give me warning?"

"Yes; not to call hard names, or mayhap I'll throw them back at you."

"Do you dare to speak to me in that manner," said the miser, "after all I've done for you?"

Tom Barley looked ruefully at his rags of clothes, and said, with unconscious humour, "Yes, you have done for me; there's no mistake about that. I remember you promised to make my fortune. I look as if it was made!"

"And whose fault is it," said Miser Farebrother, "that you're a pauper—whose fault but your own? That is, if what you say is true. But it isn't. You've got money rolled up in bundles somewhere—my money, that you've robbed me of."

Tom Barley burst out laughing. "Who has told you that cock-and-bull?" he asked. "I'd like to give him half to prove it. I'm thinking of buying Buckingham Palace, I am. I've got money enough to pay for it rolled up in bundles."

"Hold your tongue," said the miser, "and listen to me."

"Go ahead," said Tom Barley.

"When I first took you into my service," the miser commenced—

"At twopence a week," interposed Tom. "The Bank of England's breaking down with my savings."

"It was my intention to make a man of you," continued the miser; and again Tom Barley interrupted him.

"The Lord Almighty did that while you was thinking of it."

"But," proceeded the miser, "I soon found out that I had taken a hopeless case in hand; I soon discovered that a clodhopper you were and a clodhopper you would remain, till you took your place in the workhouse as a regular. Then I lost interest in you, and let you go your way."

"In a minute or two," said Tom Barley, "I've got a couple of words to say to you that I don't go out of this room without saying."

"I allowed you to remain on my estate, and gave you your meals, and paid you so much a week."

"Why not say so little, instead of so much?" asked Tom, who, driven by necessity and despair, was coming out in a new light.

"The work you did I could have had done for a song—"

"The Lord forbid," said Tom, "that I should have heard you sing it! It would have given me the gripes. I've got 'em now."

"But I kept you on out of charity, and I told you that you were at liberty to earn money elsewhere whenever you could pick up an odd job."

"My experience is," he said, "that there's about five million evens to one odd."

"The result of my kindness and liberality is that you are as you are, an idle, skulking, thieving vagabond."

"Have you done?" asked Tom.

"Not yet. I have had a serious complaint made against you, and I intend to take notice of it in a practical way. You have threatened the life of my clerk, Mr. Jeremiah Pamflett, a most estimable young man, in whom I place implicit confidence. You lie in ambush for him, and he goes in terror of you."

"That's the best thing I've heard yet," said Tom Barley, rubbing his hands gleefully.

"Such a state of things is no longer to be endured, and I shall put an end to it. Tom Barley, I discharge you from my service."

"Is that all?"

"That is all. I wash my hands of you. As to your conduct toward my clerk, I warn you to be very careful. A watch will be set upon you, and if you repeat your threats you will have to put up with the consequences."

"I'll do that; it's a matter between this Jeremiah of yours and me. As to threatening his life, that I've never done. A long while ago I got him thrashed—I didn't do it myself; I was too big—for insulting your daughter, and if ever he insults her again, and I get to know it, he'll be thrashed again. As to being turned from your service, I'll put up with it. Whatever I do I can't be worse off than I am. But you said something else. You said I've got money rolled up in bundles somewhere, and that I've robbed you of it. Now out with it like a man; you did say it!"

"Yes, I did," snarled Miser Farebrother.

"What I've got to say to that is, that you're a liar! I

ain't given to hard words, but when I'm drove to it I use 'em ; and my answer to your charge is, you're a liar ! Straight from the shoulder, master : you're a liar !"

Upon that Tom marched out of the room, with erect head and angry eye ; but when he got half-way down the staircase his look softened and his head drooped, for Phœbe stood before him. While he was in the presence of Miser Farebrother, asserting his manhood, he had not thought of her. She had heard the angry voices of her father and Tom, and she had waited to learn the cause. She beckoned Tom to follow her, and they were presently in the little room which she could call her own.

"Oh, Tom," she said, "what is it ? "

"Well, miss," he replied, " I hardly like to say, but you'd get to know it if I didn't tell you. Your father and me's had a difference, all along of that clerk of his, Jeremiah, Mrs. Pamflett's white-livered son. He's been telling your father stories about me which ain't true. Don't believe 'em when you hear 'em—don't !"

"I won't, Tom."

"Thank you, miss. I'm going to leave Parksides, miss."

"Oh, Tom !"

"Your father's discharged me. If he hadn't, I don't know what I should have done, because—look at me, miss —I ain't fit to be seen."

"Oh, Tom, I am so sorry! How I shall miss you!"

"I feel that bad over it, because of you, that I can't express. But it ain't my fault."

"I am sure it is not, Tom. Have you thought what you shall do?"

"Well, miss, I'm going to London, to be a policeman, if they'll take me on. It ain't my idea : it's somebody else's. And perhaps if I get to be a policeman, I'll be put on somewhere near Camden Town. I don't ask for anything better, miss ; for then I shall be near where you will be sometimes, and I can look after you. Don't speak to me, miss, don't look at me, for I feel like breaking down. Good-bye, Miss Phœbe, good-bye, and God bless you!"

And, choking with tears, the honest fellow rushed away.

CHAPTER XVII.

THE visit of the Lethbridges to Parksides was an event of great importance. Neither Uncle Leth, Fanny nor Bob had ever been there, and it was five or six years since Aunt Leth had set foot in it. Of all the family she was the only one who would have been able to recognize Miser Farebrother, and to say, "That is Phœbe's father." Nearly twenty years had elapsed since Uncle Leth had seen the miser, and he was rather doubtful as to how he would be received, their last meeting not having been a pleasant one. Fanny was very curious and very nervous; Phœbe's father was a solemn mysterious personage, a being apart, whose acquaintance she was now for the first time to make. What kind of looking gentleman was he? Their albums contained the portraits of all their friends and relations, near and distant, some from infancy upward; but the portrait of

Miser Farebrother found no place therein. It is doubtful, indeed, whether he had ever had his portrait taken; certainly there was none extant. Even Phœbe did not possess one. It had been a tacit arrangement among the Lethbridge's not to refer in general conversation to Phœbe's father, and to Bob and Fanny he was an utter stranger in fact and sentiment. But now that they were to be brought into contact with him, he became an object of immediate interest to them.

"What shall we call him?" said Fanny to Bob. "Of course he is our uncle, and we ought to call him Uncle Farebrother."

Bob professed not to care — in which he was not ingenuous. "All that I've heard about him," he said, "is that he is known as Miser Farebrother."

"It won't do to call him that," said Fanny; "he would be offended, and might fly out at us. Ought I to kiss him?"

"Wait till you're asked," replied Bob. "He must be immensely rich."

"More shame for him," said Fanny indignantly, "to

keep Phœbe as short as he does. What does he do with all his money?"

"Wraps it up in old stockings, buries it, hides it in the chimneys, carries it in bags round his waist, stuffs his mattress with it. There was a miser found dead in a garret in Lambeth the other day, and though there wasn't a crust of bread in the room, they found four thousand pounds hidden away in teapots, mouse-traps, nightcaps, old boots and all sorts of rum places. He used to go about begging, and would snatch a bone from a dog."

"Miserable wretch!" cried Fanny. "I hope Uncle Farebrother isn't like that."

"Not exactly, I should say; but quite bad enough. He hasn't treated us very handsomely."

"Well, never mind," said Fanny. "We don't go to see him; we are going for Phœbe's sake."

Their anticipations of their uncle were not very glowing; but as they had been warned by their mother, what passed between them respecting him was regarded as confidential. To Phœbe they said not a word.

On the Saturday morning Mr. Lethbridge, on his way to

the bank, had a little day-dream. He and his wife and children had arrived at the railway station which led to Parksides, and had beguiled the journey by discussing how they should get to Miser Farebrother's house. Should they ride? Should they walk? Would Phœbe meet them? The question was settled for them immediately they alighted from the train. There was Phœbe, all smiles, and dressed most beautifully, even elegantly. And who should be by her side but her father, all smiles also, and elegantly dressed? He came forward in the pleasantest manner, and shook hands with every one of them, and Phœbe whispered to Uncle Leth, " It is all nonsense about father being a miser. It was only fun on his part. He has been saving up for me, and you, and Aunt Leth, and all of us. You have no idea how good and kind he is." There was actually a carriage waiting for them, and they all got into it, and rode in jubilant spirits to Parksides : a mansion fit for a nobleman. Gables, turrets, mullioned windows, walls covered with old ivy, grounds and gardens most tastefully laid out—everything perfect. Footmen about, and pretty maids neatly dressed, music playing somewhere.   There was a sumptuous dinner provided for them : wonderful dishes, the best of wine.   The day-dreamer made a speech, in which he dilated upon the happiness which Miser Farebrother had shed upon them, and how it was all the greater because of the delightful surprise which Phœbe's father had been for so many years preparing for them.   Mr. Lethbridge's mental speeches were always marvels of oratory—not a word out of place, the turns most felicitous—and this speech at Miser Farebrother's dinner-table was even happier than usual.   Then Miser Fare-brother responded, and came out in a light so unexpected and agreeable that the place rang with cheers, and the music struck up " For he's a jolly good fellow," in which they all joined at the top of their voices.   When the feast was ended Miser Farebrother asked him to step into his private room, and there, over a bottle of rare old port, he produced his will, which he read to the dreamer, and in which every member of the dreamer's family was handsomely provided for.   He would not listen to the dreamer's expressions of gratitude. " Not a word : not a word," he said.   " It has been a whim of mine to allow you to suppose I was mean and miserly and cruel, when all the time I have been overflowing with the milk of human kindness. Now we are all going to live happily together." Then they joined the young people in the grounds, where there was a marquee erected for the guests to dance in. There was quite a gathering; numbers of ladies and gentlemen had been invited, and among them Fred Cornwall, who had returned from his holiday trip. The young lawyer was dancing now with Fanny, and Miser Farebrother said: "I shouldn't wonder if that was to be a match. When it is arranged, look out for a splendid wedding present from me;" and Fanny coming up, the miser pinched her cheek, and said something which made her blush. It was altogether a most exhilarating entertainment, and the union of the relations most harmonious. Of course it was a lovely night, and as the dreamer arrived at the bank, he said to himself, "I have passed the pleasantest day in my remembrance."

While he was at his desk a conversation took place at home between Fanny and her mother respecting Fred Cornwall. He had called upon the Lethbridges on the previous evening, and although he was full of agreeable chat, he seemed disappointed at not finding Phœbe at her aunt's house. As he had said in his last letter to Fanny, he had brought presents home for all of them, and when Fanny twitted him privately with having nothing for Phœbe, he answered,

"Oh, yes, I have; but I must give them to her personally."

"To-morrow will be a capital time to give her a present," said Fanny.

"Is she coming here to-morrow?" asked Fred, eagerly.

"No," replied Fanny; "we are all going to her at Parksides. It is her birthday."

"She did not leave me an invitation, I suppose?" said Fred.

"No," said Fanny; "but if I were a young gentleman I shouldn't wait for one."

"Wouldn't you?"

"No. I should make my way to Parksides, and take my presents with me, and give her a delightful surprise."

"Do you really think I might venture?"

"*I* shouldn't think twice about it," said Fanny, vivaciously,

"But you mustn't come with us, because, of course, we don't know anything about it. We shall be quite astonished when you make your appearance with a flourish of trumpets."

There and then the affectionate conspiracy was discussed and planned, and Fred said that Fanny was the dearest girl living, which Fanny disputed, asking how could she be when Phœbe stopped the way.

It was about noon on the Saturday that Fanny said to her mother, "I am going to let you into a secret."

Aunt Leth's thoughts immediately travelled to Fred Cornwall. She had observed the whispered conference which had taken place on the previous night between the young man and her daughter, with their heads very close together, and she had formed her own conclusions; and now the secret was about to be revealed. Fred had been making serious love to Fanny; there could not be a doubt that this was Fanny's secret.

"Yes, my dear," said Mrs. Lethbridge, tenderly.

"It is about Mr. Cornwall," said Fanny.

"Yes, Fanny."

Despite her joy, a pang went right through her heart; it is always so with affectionate parents when the bolt really falls, and the contemplation of a beloved daughter leaving the happy home becomes a certainty.

"And Phœbe," said Fanny.

Mrs. Lethbridge's face underwent a change. In matters of the heart a woman's instincts are lightning-tipped.

"I have an idea," said Fanny, "that they are fond of each other."

Mrs. Lethbridge looked apprehensively at her daughter, but she saw in Fanny's face no despondency, no disappoint- ment. On the contrary, it was radiant. The fond mother smiled.

"Only an idea, Fanny?" she asked.

"Only an idea, mother," said Fanny. "There has been nothing really serious said, but I am certain I am not mis- taken. Now confess, mother; you thought I was the magnet?"

"Well, my dear, I did have a suspicion, and it has been proved to be wrong."

"You are not sorry, mother?"

"No, my dear, so long as you are happy. That is my only care."

"I am perfectly happy, and I mean to die an old maid. Dear Phœbe! I do hope everything will turn out right."

"We all hope so, Fanny. I suppose I must not say anything to her?"

"Not for worlds, mother. You must wait till she speaks to you."

"I am not so sure, Fanny. She has no mother to confide in, and to whom she can unreservedly open her heart. I must think over it, for her sake."

"If you thought Mr. Cornwall was good enough for me," said Fanny, "he is good enough for Phœbe."

"My dear, the cases are different."

"How different?"

"Mr. Cornwall knows her position. If it had been you instead of Phœbe, he would not have expected money with you. When people have arrived at the time of life which your father and I have reached, and have children whom they love as we love ours, they cannot help feeling a little disturbed at their want of fortune.   Young men nowadays look out for money; it is not as it used to be."

"It is with me, mother.   I am an old fashioned girl, and if a young man casts sheeps' eyes at me it will be a satisfaction to know that it isn't my dowry that attracts him. And for my part, mother, I mean to marry for love—if I ever *do* marry."

"I am glad to hear you say so, my dear; they are the happiest marriages.   Our life has been a happy one: never for one moment have I regretted marrying your father."

"I should think not, mother!   Who is there in the world to compare with him?"

"There is not one, my dear.   It would be difficult indeed to meet with a man so good, so unselfish, so devoted.   But we were speaking of Phœbe.   The cases are different, I said. Mr. Cornwall would have had no difficulty in obtaining our consent, had it been you instead of Phœbe.   Have you forgotten that Phœbe has a father?"

"I did not think of him," said Fanny, a little depressed by the allusion.   "But what objection could he have to Mr. Cornwall?"

" That is not for us to say. Phœbe's father is a peculiar man, and he may have views for Phœbe of which we are ignorant. Mr. Cornwall's suit will rest with him, not with us."

" Mr. Cornwall is a gentleman."

" Undoubtedly ; and, so far as I can judge, calculated to make a girl happy. But that is not the question."

" What is the question, mother ? "

" Money. Fanny, what I am about to say must not pass out of this room."

" Very well, mother."

" Phœbe's father may say to Mr. Cornwall : ' You ask me for my daughter's hand. How much money have you got ? ' "

" What a coarse way of putting it ! " exclaimed Fanny disdainfully.

" I am aware of it, but for Phœbe's sake I am trying to think it out in the way it will happen. I have never inquired into Mr. Cornwall's circumstances ; but they are not very flourishing at present, are they ? "

" I don't think they are."

" I know they are not. He and your father have had

conversations which lead me to the belief that he earns just a sufficient income to keep himself comfortably."

"He is very clever in his profession; and there is the future."

"That is one of the things I am thinking of," said Mrs. Lethbridge, gravely: "the future. 'How much money have you got?' Phœbe's father will ask him; and when the young man answers honestly—as Mr. Cornwall is sure to do—Phœbe's father will say, 'As you have no money of your own, you come after my daughter's.' I am very much afraid of it, Fanny. I pray that there is no trouble in store for her."

"Mother, you frighten me." Fanny experienced at that moment a feeling of terror at the conspiracy into which she and Fred Cornwall had entered, which was to result in Fred's unexpected appearance at Parksides with birthday presents for Phœbe. She did not dare to refer to it, so she kept the secret locked in her breast.

"I do not wish to frighten you, my dear," said Mrs. Lethbridge, "and perhaps, after all, I am only raising bugbears. Let us hope for the best."

" We will," said Fanny, brightening up instantly. She was like an April day; the least glimpse of sunshine brought gladness to her. " And now, mother, ust one word."

" Well, my dear ? "

" If Mr. Cornwall proposes to Phœbe—which he will—and if she accepts him—which she will—and if he speaks to Phœbe's father, and Phœbe's father will not hear of it, what is to be done ? "

" My dear child, you are putting a riddle to me."

" What I want to know is," said Fanny, very determinedly, " whether, if Phœbe's father refuses his consent, Phœbe ought to marry without it." She felt that she had achieved a triumph in putting it so clearly.

" Would you marry without ours ? " asked Mrs. Leth bridge.

" Mother, be logical, as Fred Cornwall says. Did you not say yourself that the cases are different ? "

" Yes, I did," replied the perplexed mother.

" Well, there it is, then," said Fanny ; and as her mother did not speak, she relentlessly opened another broadside. " If an honourable gentleman really and truly loves a young lady, and if a young lady really and truly loves him in return, and if they are worthy of each other, and if there is a fair prospect of his getting along in the world in an honourable profession, and of their being truly happy together, ought they not to marry in spite of a miserly hunks of a father?"

"My dear," said Mrs. Lethbridge, "let us drop the subject, and hope for the best."

"Thank you, mother. *We* know that Phœbe is not happy at home."

"It is so, unfortunately."

"And *we* know that our home is hers if she should ever be without one."

"Yes, my dear."

"Then, my own dearest mother," said Fanny, putting her arms round the good mother's neck and showering kisses upon her, "there is nothing more to be said."

CHAPTER XVIII.

UNCLE Leth's day-dream was not realized—but then his day-dreams never were. When he and his family, travelling third-class, reached the station for Parksides, there was no Miser Farebrother to receive them with open arms and a carriage. Phœbe was there, and that was quite as good—almost more than they expected. She was a favourite with the station-master and ticket-takers, who always admitted her to the platform, whether the gates were closed or not; and the Lethbridges, looking out of the window, saw her waving her handkerchief to them, and running along the platform, the moment they were in sight. Then there was such a kissing and hugging as made the hearts of the un-envious ones glad to witness, and the mouths of the envious ones to water, wishing they had a free ticket to participate in an entertainment so delightful.

16—2

"It *is* good of you to come and meet us," said Fanny. "I was wondering all the way whether you would."

"I did not know whether I should be able," said Phœbe, in a flutter of excitement; "but Mrs. Pamflett has been very kind. I hardly liked to ask her to help me with the tea; but she came and offered of her own accord, and said perhaps I would like to go and meet my friends. So here I am."

Mr. Lethbridge opened his ears upon mention of Mrs. Pamflett, and he was glad to hear so good an account of her. An act of thoughtfulness and good-nature from her was a guarantee for her son, who had discounted his acceptance for three hundred pounds for the dramatic author and Kiss.

They had all brought modest birthday presents for Phœbe, which they handed to her at once, with flowers and kisses and the best of affectionate wishes. Bob was in the seventh heaven in consequence of being allowed a share in the kissing business.

"I did not have time to write to you last night," whispered Fanny to Phœbe. "He has come home, and had tea with us. He is looking so well! brown, and hand-somer than ever. What a perfectly lovely day ! "

They walked to Parksides, expressing pleasure at every-thing—at the weather, at the scenery, at the pretty village, at the children, at the cottages, at the church—all of which, it seemed to the little party, had put on a holiday garb in honour of Phœbe. The flowers were brighter, the sunlight clearer, the birds sang more sweetly, as they walked and talked, each of the Lethbridges claiming a share in Phœbe's society, and each obtaining it. Now with Bob, now with Fanny, now with Aunt Leth, now with Uncle—she ran from one to another, chatting gaily, and bursting out into snatches of song. It was her day, her very own—a day of sunshine without and within.

Mrs. Pamflett's amiability needs a word of explanation. The conversation she had had with her son Jeremiah had opened her eyes as to his intentions; and both to please him and to win Phœbe's favour she had offered to assist the young girl. But for Jeremiah's sake she would not have dreamt of such a thing. She had lain awake half the night thinking of the conversation, and she had come to the con-

.clusion that it would be a fine match for Jeremiah. Much as she had disliked Phœbe, she admired her son for his ambition. Miser Farebrother's "aching of bones" was growing worse every week, every day; suffering as he did, it would soon be impossible for him to give any personal attention to his business in London. No one understood it, no one could attend to it, but Jeremiah. What, then, was more feasible than Jeremiah's scheme of becoming Miser Farebrother's son-in-law? "To think," she mused in the night, "that it never entered my mind! But Jeremiah's got a head on him. He will be a millionaire, and I shall be a lady!" The idea of a repulse—that Phœbe would not think Jeremiah good enough for her—never occurred to Mrs. Pamflett; if it had, she would have rejected it with scorn. What! her son, her bright boy—handsome, shrewd, and clever—not good enough for the best lady in the land! A little chit like Phœbe might consider herself lucky that such a man as Jeremiah should condescend to her. "I can't, for the life of me, see," she mused, "why Jeremiah should be so taken with her; but there's no accounting for a man's fancies. And then he said he wasn't particular. Ah! Jeremiah knows what he's about." All her hopes, all her desires, all her ambitions, being centred in her bright boy, she determined to assist him by every means in her power. She commenced the next morning, on this happy birthday, and, to Phœbe's surprise, wished her a happy birthday and many returns of them, and offered to relieve the young girl of all responsibility in the preparing of the tea for her friends. Phœbe met her advances gladly. On such a day no suspicion of sinister motives could occur to a nature so sweet, so pure, so innocent; and when Mrs. Pamflett asked her to accept a brooch, she received it with a pleasant feeling of gratitude. "It is an old brooch," Mrs. Pamflett said, "a memento; and although it is not very valuable, it comes from my heart." There was a certain literal truth in this, because the brooch was one which Mrs. Pamflett was in the habit of wearing; it might not have been considered a very suitable gift for a young girl like Phœbe, as it contained a lock of some dead-and-gone person's hair, arranged as a feather or a curl over a tombstone. Once upon a time it doubtless had a meaning, and might have brought a light of joy or sorrow to special human eyes; but the memories which sanctified it being deader than the deadest ghost that superstition could conjure up, it certainly could not be considered a suitable gift for Phœbe. Its fatal meaning for her lay in the future.

When Mrs. Pamflett said to Phœbe that perhaps she would like to go and meet her friends at the railway station, she thought it likely that Jeremiah would be in the train. He had not told her by which train he was coming, and her desire was to give him an opportunity of walking home with Phœbe. She did not betray herself when she saw Phœbe return in the company of the Lethbridges and without Jeremiah. She possessed a gift invaluable to sly, secretive natures—the gift of absolute self-repression. Phœbe introduced Mrs. Pamflett to her friends. Aunt Leth was already acquainted with her, and was astonished at the graciousness and amiability of the house-keeper, her previous experience of her having been quite the reverse. Uncle Leth nodded and said, "How d'ye do?" but Fanny was rather stiff—"uppish," as Mrs. Pamflett subsequently told her son.

"Tea will not be ready for half an hour or so," said Mrs.

Pamflett, aside, to Phœbe. " I have set it upstairs in your favourite room."

" O," was Phœbe's delighted rejoinder, "how kind of you!"

" I want you to love me," said Mrs. Pamflett. " If you find that my only wish is to please you, perhaps you will."

" Indeed I will," said Phœbe ; and thought, "Perhaps my father will love me too."

She asked the Lethbridges to wait a moment or two, and she went to her father's room.

" Aunt and uncle are here, and my cousins."

" What has that to do with me ? " he asked.

" May they come up and see you, father ? "

" No," he replied ; "I can't be bothered. They wish to see me as little as I wish to see them."

While this last question was being asked and answered, Mrs. Pamflett entered the room.

"I think you should see them, sir," she said.

" Why ? " he asked.

" As a mark of politeness," said Mrs. Pamflett. " Mr. Lethbridge and your nephew and niece have never been here before, and they might think it rude of you."

"Do I care if they do?" he snarled.

"It is not that," she answered, calmly, "but it is Miss Phœbe's birthday."

"Mrs. Pamflett is very kind," said Phœbe, nervously, "but if you don't wish, father—"

"I wish to do what is right," he said, very coolly, as was his habit when he was opposed.

"We all know that," said Mrs. Pamflett, in a voice as composed as his own. "You always do what is right. Mr. and Mrs. Lethbridge and their children are going to have tea with Miss Phœbe in honour of her birthday, and I have been getting it ready, and am going to wait on them. You ought to join them. I have set a chair for you at the head of the table."

"Oh, father, if you would!" implored Phœbe, clasping her hands.

"You wish it?" he asked of her, but not removing his eyes from Mrs. Pamflett's face.

"Yes, father. If you would only be so good!"

"And *you* wish it?" he asked of Mrs. Pamflett.

"For Miss Phœbe's sake I do," replied Mrs.

Pamflett, without so much as winking an eyelid.

" Not for your own ? "

" I have told you what I think."

" Let it be so," said Miser Farebrother.   " Phœbe, I will take tea with you and your friends."

" Oh, papa ! "   In her gratitude the affectionate girl— only too ready to give love for love—threw her arms round her father's neck and kissed him.

" There ! there ! " he said, pushing her away ; " go down to your friends.   You can stop, Mrs. Pamflett."

Phœbe ran down-stairs to convey the good news to the Lethbridges, and Mrs. Pamflett and the miser were left together.

" Now, Mrs. Pamflett," he said abruptly, " what is all this about ? "

" I do not understand you," was her reply.

" You understand me thoroughly," he said.   " I can't see through a millstone, but I can see through you."

" Then why do you ask me to explain anything? " she retorted.

" You have lived here sixteen years," he said, " and you

think you know me as well as I am sure I know you. Because I have never interfered with you, because I have allowed you to do as you like—"

She interrupted him here. "Have I ever wasted a penny of your money?"

"To my knowledge, no. If you had, you would have heard of it."

"Yes, that is very certain. Every farthing spent in this house has been accounted for in the book which you look over every week. You would find it hard to get anybody in my place."

"Oh, that is it! You threaten to leave me!"

"You are not only mistaken, you know you are stating an untruth. Yes, an untruth." The words denoted in-dignation, but it was not expressed in her voice or manner.

"Is that a proper way to speak to me?" he cried.

"I pass no opinion," was her unimpassioned reply. "If you are tired of me, or if I do not please you, you can send me away."

"You would go?"

"I should be bound to go. What else could I do? If I refused, you could call in the police."

"You are bent upon exasperating me, I see. You know I could not do without you."

"I know it."

"And that is why you are impudent to me."

"You have never found me so."

"Because I am bound to you hand and foot, because you know my ways, having grown into them, because I depend upon you and trust you, because I am weak and ill and dependent, you think you can twist me about as you like. You shall find that you are mistaken."

"Do you wish me to leave Parksides to-night? I will go and get ready."

He glared at her. "Well, why don't you go?"

"I am waiting for orders. Give them, and I will obey you—as I have obeyed you in everything else."

"You have no more wish to leave me," he said, laughing scornfully, "than I have that you should. You could no more do without me than I could do without you."

"There may be a balance," she said, "and it may be to my credit. You seem to be angry because I have made an endeavour to please your daughter."

"Have you ever endeavoured to please her before to-day?" he asked slyly.

"Have you," she retorted, "ever taken the trouble to ascertain?"

He paused awhile before he spoke. "Having been imprisoned up here, out of sight of things, with no eyes for anything beyond this room, you may think I haven't known what is going on in my house. You are mistaken—egregiously mistaken—as mistaken as your son Jeremiah, who perhaps has an idea that I do not know when I am absent what is going on in my office in London."

"Do you wish *him* to leave as well as me?" said Mrs. Pamflett. The conspicuous and amazing feature of her speech was that she made these propositions as though they did not in the slightest degree affect her, or any person in whom she was interested. "With his talents for business, he will not have the least difficulty in obtaining a position of trust elsewhere."

"I have unmasked you," said Miser Farebrother; "you have a design. Out with it."

"I have no design," said Mrs. Pamflett, "except your interests; and if it happens that your interests and ours—"

"And ours!" he cried.

"And ours," she repeated. "If it happens that our interests are identical, it should rather please than anger you. You say that you are bound hand and foot to me. That is a compliment, and I am obliged to you; but supposing it to be true, I am as much bound hand and foot to you, and so is my son Jeremiah. It may be in your power to so chain him to you that he would become an absolute slave to your interests."

"Interests again!" he exclaimed, impatiently. "Always interests—nothing but interests."

"Well," said Mrs. Pamflett, "what do we live for? What do *you* live for?"

This was a home thrust indeed, and Miser Farebrother accepted it in good part. Despite the outward aspect of this singular conversation, it was not entirely disagreeable to him. He appreciated the services of Mrs. Pamflett and her son ; he knew that he could not replace them ; he had not left it to the present hour to reckon up their monetary value.

"To come back to Phœbe," he said ; "what is all this about?   No beating about the bush—plain speaking."

"I love her," said Mrs. Pamflett, "as a daughter."

"And Jeremiah is your only son ? "

"My only son.   The best, the brightest, the cleverest man in England !   And devoted to you, body and soul."

"I am infinitely obliged to you," said Miser Farebrother, with a malicious grin ; "I will think about it."

CHAPTER XIX.

A BEAUTIFUL BIRTHDAY.

MISER FAREBROTHER did not keep his promise of taking tea with Phœbe and her friends—he had matter more serious to occupy him—but to some extent he made atonement for it. He sent for Phœbe, and told her that he did not feel equal to the excitement, but that, before the evening was over, he would welcome Mr. and Mrs. Lethbridge and her cousins to Parksides. This, to Phœbe, was almost as good as the keeping of his promise; he spoke in a feeble voice, as though he was ill, and his unexpected kindness and consideration touched her. She put her hand timidly upon his shoulder, moved thereto by sweet pity for his condition, and he did not repulse her; she was even bold enough to lower her face to his and kiss him more than once, and he bore it contentedly. A new feeling stirred her heart, new hopes were born within her. That this unexpected change in her father's bearing toward her should take place on her birthday was a happy omen, and she was deeply grateful for it. From this time forth her home life would bring her joy instead of sorrow. She went from her father's room with a light step, ready to burst forth into song.

The feeble voice in which Miser Farebrother had spoken to Phœbe was assumed; his weakness was assumed; all the time she was with him he was watching her keenly and warily. He had never thought of her but as a child; the idea of her marrying had never entered his head; but now that it was presented to him he seized upon it and turned it about to the light. The only friends his daughter had were the Lethbridges; they had a son, who doubtless would be only too ready to snap at such a bait as Phœbe. For her sake?—because he loved her?—not at all. Because her father was supposed to be rich; because of the money he would calculate upon getting with her. And thereafter there would ever and eternally be but one cry—money, money, money! All their arts, all their endeavours, their only object, would be to bleed his money-bags bare. "No, no, Mr. Lethbridge," thought Miser Farebrother, "not a penny shall ever pass from my pockets to yours." But the danger might not present itself through the Lethbridges. Phœbe might fall in love with a spendthrift or a cunning rogue. That would be as bad—worse, perhaps. Despite his aversion to the Lethbridges, his experience of them had taught him that they were proud, and that in the event of Phœbe marrying into their family there would be a chance of respite for him after a time, a chance that they would make up their minds to submit to poverty, and trouble him no more. With a spendthrift it would be different. There would be no peace for him ; the appeals for money would be incessant ; he would be torn to pieces with worry. Then came the cunning rogue on to the scene, in the shape which was most objectionable to Miser Farebrother, in that of a scheming lawyer. There was more to fear from that than from any other aspect of the subject. Miser Farebrother knew the power of the law when he invoked it on his side—which he never did without being prepared with stamped deeds and witnessed signatures— but he knew also the power of the law if, in certain cases which he could call to mind, it were invoked against him.

17—2

Plaintiff and defendant were different things, had different chances. He himself never prosecuted without weighing the minutest chance, without being absolutely certain that he was standing on sure legal ground. He had submitted to losses rather than run a risk. There was one instance in which a disreputable, out-at-elbows, dissipated lawyer had defied him to his teeth—had unblushingly defrauded him by threatening exposure. Miser Farebrother, knowing that certain transactions in which he was principal would not bear the light, had submitted to be robbed rather than be dragged into the witness-box and cross-examined. Such inquiries often commence tamely, but there is no saying where they lead to; a man's smallest peccadilloes are shamelessly dragged forth, his very soul is turned inside out. Then there are judges who, the moment a money-lending case comes before them, set to work on the debtor's side to defraud the creditor. Miser Farebrother, therefore, was wise in his generation in the tactics he pursued. Some low-minded scheming limb of the law might pay court to Phœbe, with but one end in view. The thought of it sent a shiver through his nerves.

His reflections were not agreeable, but he had a large amount of common-sense, and he knew they might be serviceable. He was not displeased with Mrs. Pamflett for suggesting them. She was a useful woman; truly, as he had said, he would not have known what to do without her. She had made the same admission on her side; that was honest of her. There were conditions of life which a sensible man must accept and make the best of, and his was one. Not being able to purchase a new set of bones and nerves, he felt that to a great extent he was at the mercy of Mrs. Pamflett and Jeremiah. As difficult to replace the loss of Jeremiah in his London office as to replace the loss of Mrs. Pamflett in his house at Parksides. It was a wretched state of things, but it must be borne, and as much profit as possible made out of it. " Phœbe had only herself to blame," he thought, with monstrous mental distortion. "If she had been a boy instead of a girl, it would all have been different."

There was no mistaking the meaning of Mrs. Pamflett's references to her son. Well, Phœbe might do worse : and if, as Mrs. Pamflett had said, he could so bind Jeremiah to him as to make him an absolute slave to his interests, such a marriage might be altogether the best thing that could happen. It would be an additional protection to Miser Farebrother's money-bags. "I will bind him tight," thought the miser—"tight! Clever lad, Jeremiah; but I shall be a match for him."

Not a thought of his daughter's happiness; she would have to do as he ordered. Thus, in the secrecy of Miser Farebrother's room, the web was forming in which Phœbe was to be entangled and her happiness wrecked.

Outside this room everything was bright. Phœbe had told Aunt and Uncle Leth of her father's goodness, and they, simple-minded and guileless as herself, rejoiced with her. "Upon my word," said Uncle Leth, "it almost makes my dream true. Phœbe moved about, singing, smiling, laughing to herself now and then, and scattering flowers of gladness all around her. "I never saw our dear Phœbe so bright," said Aunt Leth. "Our visit to Parksides is a most beautiful surprise, quite different from what I expected."

It was not the only surprise; there was another, even more subtly sweet to Phœbe. This was the appearance of Fred Cornwall, who, finding no bell at the gates by which he could announce his arrival, walked boldly through, and suddenly presented himself. They were all outside the house, awaiting Mrs. Pamflett's summons to tea.

"Why," exclaimed the arch-conspirator Fanny, calling astonishment into her features, "if there isn't Mr. Cornwall coming up the walk! Who would have thought it? and how ever did he find us out?"

Phœbe turned toward the young man, blushing, and with a palpitating heart.

"I hope you will pardon the liberty I have taken," said he; "but as it is your birthday I thought I might venture."

"How did you know?" asked Phœbe, her hand in his.

"A little bird told me," was his reply. "How do you do, Aunt Leth? How do you do, Miss Fanny?"

He exchanged pleasant words of greeting with his friends and looked very handsome, and by no means ill at

ease, though an uninvited guest. Well dressed, well man-
nered, a gentleman every inch of him.

At the door of the house, unseen by anyone of the happy
group, Mrs. Pamflett appeared. She saw the meeting, and
noted Phœbe's blushing face. She partly closed the door,
and, retreating a step, stood there, watching and debating
within herself.

Fred Cornwall held in his hand a bunch of flowers, very
choice specimens, loosely tied, and arranged with charming
grace. Not in the shape of a regulation bouquet, but infinitely more beautiful in their apparently careless form.
He offered them to Phœbe, and she accepted them. Mrs.
Pamflett set her thin white lips close.

Then the young gentleman presented, as birthday gifts,
the presents he had bought for Phœbe on his Continental
trip, accompanying them with heart-felt wishes. Phœbe,
trembling, thrilling, was in the seventh heaven of joy.

When, however, she recovered her self-possession, she
felt herself in a difficulty. Would her father be angry?
Aunt Leth, seeing the light shadow on her face, moved aside
with her.

"You are thinking of your father, Phœbe?" she said.

"Yes, aunt."

"You would like Mr. Cornwall to stop to tea?" Enlightened by Fanny's confession in the early part of the day, she regarded Mr. Cornwall and her niece as lovers, and her sympathies were already enlisted on their side.

"Yes, aunt," replied Phœbe. "But it is a little awkward, is it not? What shall I do?"

"Go and ask your father," said Aunt Leth. "Say that Mr. Cornwall is a friend of ours, and that you have often met him at our house. Go at once; Mr. Cornwall need not know; I will keep him engaged while you are away."

Phœbe nodded, and started for the house. Mrs. Pamflett, seeing her coming, beat a retreat, not desiring to meet the young girl just at that moment.

"Father," said Phœbe, "I am in a difficulty. I hope you will not mind."

"Not at all," said Miser Farebrother. She had never heard him speak in a voice so kind and gentle.

"A friend of Aunt Leth's has just arrived, and has brought me these." She showed him the flowers and the presents, and he pretended to take interest in them. "He has been on the Continent, father; and he purchased presents for all of us."

"Very generous, very generous," said Miser Farebrother. "Did you invite him here?"

"No, father; I would not have dared without asking your consent. I can't make out how he found his way here, and how he knew it was my birthday. I did not tell him."

"Perhaps your aunt did."

"I think not, father."

"What is your difficulty, Phœbe?"

"I should like to ask him to stop to tea, if you have no objection."

"You may ask him," said Miser Farebrother. He had a direct motive in giving his consent so readily. The nature of his late reflections had inspired an interest in all Phœbe's acquaintances, and he wished to see this friend of her aunt's.

"Oh, father, how can I thank you?"

"By obeying me, Phœbe."

"Yes, father; I will."

"I hope you will keep your word. What is the name of this new friend ? "

" Not new, father—old."

" New to me. What is his name? "

" Mr. Cornwall. He is a gentleman, father."

"Young?"

" Yes, father."

" What is he besides being a gentleman ? "

" He is a barrister."

" A lawyer? Ah! A clever one ? "

" They say so, father."

"Ah! Is he a great friend of your aunt's ? "

" A very great friend, father. They think the world of him."

He nodded, and dismissed her, and then gave himself up again to contemplation of the incident in connection with what had preceded it. He, as well as Mrs. Pamflett, had noted his daughter's blushes, her eagerness, her excitement of delight, and he placed his own construction upon her manner. It seemed to him as if he had been drawn into some game which it was vitally necessary he should win. It was strange how things appeared to fit in with one another! He had been thinking of lawyers, and here was one in his house, an unmistakable intruder, with flowers and presents for Phœbe, the daughter of rich Miser Farebrother. A clever lawyer too, and a great friend of the Lethbridges, whom he hated from the bottom of his heart. Bold schemers they, and a bold ally this Mr. Cornwall, to pre-sume to come, uninvited, to his house, regarding him, its owner, as a person of no importance, whose wishes it was unnecessary to consult! What had passed between this un-welcome guest and Phœbe? How far had they gone? and what was being hidden from him? He did not doubt now that the presence of the Lethbridges in Parksides on his daughter's birthday was part of a cunning plot, in which their lawyer friend was a principal actor. "They are all in a league against me," he thought; "but I shall be equal with them. If Phœbe disobeys me, she must take the conse-quences. I will wring a promise from her to-night before I go to bed."

"Mr. Cornwall," said Phœbe, when she rejoined her

friends in the open, " will you stop and have a cup of tea with us."

" Would it be possible," he said, turning with smiles to Fanny, " for me to refuse ? "

" How should I know ? " said Fanny, tossing her head.

" It will be a great pleasure to me," said Fred Cornwall to Phœbe. " I almost feared that I should be looked upon as an intruder."

" Of course you did," said Fanny, making a face at him behind her cousin's back ; " that is why you came."

" We can all go back to London together," said Aunt Leth.

" Yes," said Fanny, "and you can make love to me in the train."

" You must not mind her, Mr. Cornwall," said Aunt Leth ; "her high spirits sometimes run away with her."

" I wish some nice young gentleman would," whispered Fanny to Phœbe. " Why doesn't a fairy godmother take me in hand ? "

" Aunt," said Phœbe, aside, to Mrs. Lethbridge, " I think

I was never quite so happy as I am to-day. You have no idea how kind papa has been to me."

Aunt Leth pressed Phœbe's arm affectionately, and at that moment Mrs. Pamflett appeared and said that tea was ready. She had delayed it till the last minute in the hope that Jeremiah would arrive, and she was vexed and disappointed at his absence. Outwardly, however, she was all graciousness, and she took especial pains to put on her most amiable manners.

"No girl ever had a more beautiful birthday," thought Phœbe, as they all trooped into the house.

END OF VOL. I.

PRINTED BY
KELLY AND CO., GATE STREET, LINCOLN'S INN FIELDS, W.C.;
AND MIDDLE MILL, KINGSTON-ON-THAMES.

www.ingramcontent.com/pod-product-compliance
Lightning Source LLC
Chambersburg PA
CBHW021054030726
47496CB00006B/1839